# FRIENDS
# OF ACPL

# The Green Flash

A small self-contained child who dreams reality; the ghost of a love-struck, bicycle-riding night watchman; a canary who bears an acute resemblance to the younger sister of Charles II; an old lady, hard of hearing, almost blind, but with a murderous sense of smell—these are just a few of the characters you'll encounter in this spine-tingling, mind-boggling collection by Joan Aiken.

The impact of the tales is varied and ranges all the way from grisly horror through old-fashioned mystery to comic fantasy. It's a book to curl up with and enjoy on a dark, rainy night, a book which continues to astound from the first page to the very last.

# The Green Flash

## and other tales of horror, suspense, and fantasy

### Joan Aiken

S

HOLT, RINEHART AND WINSTON
New York    Chicago    San Francisco

## Acknowledgement

The stories appearing in this collection have first been published in England in the following books and periodicals: *Argosy*, *Fontana Horror Book*, *New Statesman*, *John Bull*, *Woman's Journal*, and *The Windscreen Weepers* by Joan Aiken.

1617049

*For Charles Schlessiger*

## Books by Joan Aiken

*For young readers*

Night Fall
Smoke from Crowell's Time
A Necklace of Raindrops
The Whispering Mountain
Armitage, Armitage, Fly Away Home
Nightbirds on Nantucket
Black Hearts in Battersea
The Wolves of Willoughby Chase

*For adults*

The Embroidered Sunset
The Crystal Crow
The Fortune Hunters
Dark Interval
Beware of the Bouquet
The Silence of Herondale

# Table of Contents

# The Green Flash

# Mrs. Considine

The shop smelled of wet bricks; also of all the things in the thick square drawers—semolina, ground rice, almond flour, dried apricots, coffee; also of burlap; also of bacon, kerosene, and polish; also of damp clothes.

Julia stood gazing at the bricks on the floor, all different. Some were worn inward to a smooth curve, others bulged upward. One or two had a sort of gathering on them; she was familiar with them all, and with the knotholes along the edge of the counter, polished by leaning customers. She put her finger into a hole that exactly fitted and stood humming tunelessly, a freckled compact child in a green coat and trousers, spelling

1

out to herself the words on the shiny red weighing machine "Berkel Auto Scale," and the entrancing names on the long row of glass candy jars—Satin Cushions, Orchard Drops, Raspberry Noyau, Almond Brittle, Glacier Mints.

"And this is Julia." Her mother gently urged her forward with a hand on her shoulder.

"Why," Mrs. Considine said in her soft Irish voice, "I thought at first you were a little boy."

Julia took no notice of Mrs. Considine. All her attention was focused on the large dog with long yellow and white hair who now stood up and strolled forward from the dark end of the shop.

"Julia's rather frightened of dogs, I'm afraid," her mother explained.

"Ah now, you mustn't be that," Mrs. Considine said, laying a hand on Julia's head. "Rufus wouldn't like that now, he's as gentle as a lamb. And so you're coming down to me to learn how to make French knots?"

"Yes," said Julia shyly, but she was looking at Rufus. She had a recurring nightmare, from which she woke sweating and shaking in a transport of fear, unable to move her tongue enough to call for help. The dream was of a huge black dog with eyes like hot coals and lunatic teeth, spiked like two ranges of mountains one above the other. He advanced on her slowly down a narrow gully, howling dreadfully, while she stood paralyzed and unable to move.

But last night there had been an interruption to the dream: down the side of the ravine had bounded a rescuer, a plumy, lemon and white heraldic animal with a long pointed face and feathery tail, who had driven away the terror; and now, looking at Rufus, she recognized in him the animal of her dream. To her mother's unspeakable astonishment she went forward and placed a hand on his head, while he stared at her out of wise golden eyes.

"That's the girl," approved Mrs. Considine. "Now are you coming back with me and Rufus to tea?"

"Yes, please," said Julia, and her mother could only gaze with wonder as her morose, bashful child went off without a glance back, happily following Mrs. Considine.

The house was at the bottom of the hill; through a tunnel of trees; large, laurel-covered and hideous; Victorian, with heavy gabling, timbering, and piping, all painted a thick, dusty terra-cotta; but inside it seemed full of peace and light. Almost everything was yellow or blue, and there was a delicious smell of wool and handwoven material, raffia, straw, and wholemeal baking. The very food was yellowish in color, possibly because it was vegetarian and contained a lot of nuts.

Soon Julia's mother began to grumble that she was never at home; she really *must* come back to lunch and not stay at Mrs. Considine's whenever she went for a lesson. Julia made promises, but she forgot them every time.

It was not for some weeks that Julia began to take note of Mrs. Considine as a person, apart from the extraordinary feeling of comfort, power, and calm that she radiated; then she became apparent as a smallish, stocky woman, white-haired, dressed always in rather flowing blue clothes with thick stockings and black strapped shoes. Her eyes were brilliant triangles of blue, and she was never without a piece of handwork in her tiny, worn hands—woollen flowers, raffia mats, beading—or she would sit hunched up like a wise woman at a spinning wheel, working the treadle with her foot while her fingers twirled the long amorphous bundle of wool into a thin, regular thread.

3

Julia meanwhile sat on her footstool with her embroidery and listened to Mrs. Considine's remarks which sparked out from time to time, bright and pungent as squibs.

One morning when Julia walked into the house with her satchel of sewing, Mrs. Considine was not sitting, as was customary, in the big bay window. Guided by the sound of voices Julia went to the kitchen, warm, tiled, and spotless, where she found Ivy, the maid, sitting with her head pillowed on her arms on the kitchen table and one foot resting on a stool while Mrs. Considine gravely considered it.

"Ye'll be mad if ye dance on that," she pronounced. "Mad, I'm telling ye!"

"I've got to go," Ivy said dully. "I've just got to." She raised her face, and Julia saw that it was smudged with tears.

"Will the young man not wait?" Mrs. Considine inquired with irony.

"No he won't!" Ivy retorted. "Ruth's out to get him, and she will too, if I'm not there. Don't you see? I've got to be there." She gazed at Mrs. Considine with as pleading an expression as her usually sulky, brooding face could muster.

"Well," said Mrs. Considine thoughtfully, holding the ankle. "I'll give it a bit of a rub now, and we'll drive into Ledenham this afternoon and buy you a pair of flat-heeled shoes, which will be better than those foolish things you wear, and maybe 'twill serve. But mind you, it's pure foolishness, and if you take my advice you'll not dance—sit out with the young man on the balcony if there is one." She darted a blue, sideways flash at Ivy.

"Oh yes, I will," Ivy promised, fervent in her gratitude, her pale face strained with hope. Julia then noticed that Ivy's straight brown hair, which usually gave her a clear-cut, Joan-of-

4

Arc appeal, had been frizzed up into meaningless kinky curls, completely altering the appearance of her face.

They took Julia with them on the trip to Ledenham, and she watched while Ivy, fretfully following Mrs. Considine's exhortations, bought a pair of white, flat satin shoes. "They'll do for ye're wedding as well," Mrs. Considine remarked. The sight of them, narrow and gleaming in the tissued box, reminded Julia of her previous night's dream: she had seen Ivy dancing with white feet in the church. Mrs. Considine sat watching her remotely from a pew, and Julia noticed that Ivy's feet dripped blood; she was dancing on knife blades like the Little Mermaid.

A week later Ivy was displaying a sapphire engagement ring, given her by Dick Shepherd, the baker's delivery boy.

"Did ye sit out with him on the balcony?" asked Mrs. Considine, surveying it with benevolent irony.

"He drove me home in the van to save my ankle," Ivy replied shortly.

Mrs. Considine lent her house for the wedding reception. which was very splendid. Julia was bridesmaid with Ruth, Ivy's sister, in mauve chiffon and a silver headband deplored by Julia's mother. Champagne flowed, but Julia thought she had never known before that an atmosphere could be so bright and glittering with hate.

It was plain that the bride's and groom's families detested one another, as they milled about, shining in their satins and plummy-dark best suits. Ruth never spoke at all, but kept her pale gaze undeviatingly on the groom. Ivy looked sulky and unhappy in her white dress and green leaves; she and Dick seemed to be tied together by distrust and dislike; she followed him everywhere with a suspicious eye.

THE GREEN FLASH

Julia overheard a conversation between Mrs. Considine and the vicar.

"Thank you indeed for the altar cloth," he was saying. "You and your ladies have done a splendid piece of work."

"Oh, 'twas a trifle." She brushed his thanks aside. "It's a good thing for the women of the village to get together on something—no matter what."

"And when am I going to see you in the church admiring it?" he asked teasingly.

"When I'm in me coffin." Her emphatic tone impressed Julia, who, when she thought about it, could not ever remember seeing Mrs. Considine in church, save in her dream.

"Aren't you afraid of going to hell, dear lady?"

"Faith, no. Don't talk such nonsense to me. Why should I be when there's no such place? Or heaven either, for that matter. And don't pretend to look shocked at me, Mr. Dale, you know my views."

"I shall have the laugh of you when they let you in up there just the same."

She shook her head at him reprovingly before moving off to talk to Ivy's mother.

Ivy was to stay on working for Mrs. Considine at first after her marriage; but she was never the same girl again. She became more and more moody and bad-tempered, and Julia gave up helping in the kitchen and instead went out to chat with old Wickenden the gardener. It was coming on for flower show time, and he was in his annual frenzy of preparation, complicated by the fact that this year the rheumatism in his hands was very bad, and he found it harder and harder to work.

Julia came across him in the garden one day, almost weeping with vexation at his incapacity, and Mrs. Considine

6

was holding his hands and scrutinizing them with her usual grave attention.

"It's the dahlias, ma'am," he was saying. "I can bear all but to be beaten in my dahlias, that have always taken first prize. They say that new Mr. Gillies at the Red House is main keen on winning with his; he's put in electric heating in the glasshouses, and they've got two-three men there in all. Oh, I do feel it bad, not being able to work as I used."

"You mustn't mind it too much, Mr. Wickenden," Mrs. Considine said. "We all have to get old some time. But I'll give those hands a bit of a rub, and see if I can do something for them, for this summer at least. If you could get the dahlia cup once more, would that content you?"

On the evening before the show Julia helped Mr. Wickenden take his exhibits up to the village hall, which already had a fine smell from the heaped prize vegetables: enormous pearly onions, piles of potatoes scrubbed till they shone, monstrous pale marrows, massed greenery, the floral arrangements by members of the Women's Union, and the huge bunches of wildflowers picked by schoolchildren. Mr. Wickenden's dahlias, frilly and fluted, lemon, white, and brick-colored, were given a place of honor, and Julia, sniffing their bitter autumnal scent, thought how queer they were, unlike the real flowers, the roses and sweetpeas carefully arranged in their cut-glass vases.

That night she had a dream of Mr. Wickenden, who was lying on his back, smiling his thoughtful smile with which he used to contemplate any fine garden product. "Ah, that's grand, that is," feeling with an earthy thumb the firm, rose-colored texture of a tomato. "But we'll do better next year."

He was being carried straight upward by four angels, dressed in robes as formally fluted as the petals of the dahlias, and with great wings of the same soft brick red, that fell about him like the curtains of a four-poster. As the angels lifted him, the trowel fell from his hands and tinkled at Julia's feet.

She remembered this dream when, smiling broadly with pleasure, Mr. Wickenden went up to the platform the next afternoon to receive his first prize. He took the silver cup in both hands and then suddenly his face began to work, the cup pitched from his grasp, and he turned around and fell in a huddled heap of black broadcloth at Sir Godfrey's feet. There was consternation; the members of the committee rushed to pick him up; but he was already dead.

Mrs. Considine never fully recovered from Wickenden's death. Julia went home with her that evening, but left her at the command: "Run along, let you now, child. Good night to ye." Julia cast several anxious glances at the huddled figure wringing its hands in the shadowed windowseat.

Though she continued going down for lessons, Julia could see that Mrs. Considine's stockiness was becoming frailty, her eyes burned darker in a whiter, more furrowed face, and her hands were becoming like tiny claws. She seemed remote, never approaching Julia or touching her, though plainly the visits gave her pleasure, and Julia still sometimes, though more occasionally, stayed to a meal of nut rissoles, dry wholemeal scones, and dandelion salad.

One night Julia had a dream about Mrs. Considine.

Erect, square-shouldered as of old, she was walking confidently away along a narrow path. Presently she reached a pair of dark gates; pausing a moment before them in the gloom she considered them, and then knocked briskly, and when they opened went through without a backward glance.

Next morning Julia was half afraid, half longing for the

8

time of her lesson to come. What had the dream meant? What would Mrs. Considine be doing?

She started five minutes early running down the hill, and the telephone call just missed her. Her mother, turning from the telephone with a shocked exclamation, heard the sound of Julia's footsteps clattering away down the hill, beneath the heavy trees.

# Marmalade Wine

"Paradise,"     Blacker
said to himself, moving forward into the wood. "Paradise.
Fairyland."

He was a man given to exaggeration; poetic license he
called it, and his friends called it "Blacker's little flights of
fancy," or something less polite, but on this occasion he spoke
nothing but the truth. The wood stood silent about him, tall,
golden, with afternoon sunlight slanting through the half-
unfurled leaves of early summer. Underfoot, anemones palely
carpeted the ground. A cuckoo called.

"Paradise," Blacker repeated, closed the gate behind
him, and strode down the overgrown path, looking for a spot in

which to eat his ham sandwich. Hazel bushes thickened at either side until the circular blue eye of the gateway by which he had come in dwindled to a pinpoint and vanished. The taller trees over-topping the hazels were not yet in full leaf and gave little cover; it was very hot in the wood and very still.

Suddenly Blacker stopped short with an exclamation of surprise and regret: lying among the dog's-mercury by the path was the body of a pheasant in the full splendor of its spring plumage. Blacker turned the bird over with the townsman's pity and curiosity at such evidence of nature's unkindness; the feathers, purple-bronze, green, and gold, were as smooth under his hand as a girl's hair.

"Poor thing," he said aloud, "what can have happened to it?"

He walked on, wondering if he could turn the incident to account. "Threnody for a Pheasant in May." Too precious? Too sentimental? Perhaps a weekly would take it. He began choosing rhymes, staring at his feet as he walked, abandoning his conscious rapture at the beauty around him.

Stricken to death . . . and something . . . leafy ride,
Before his . . . something . . . fully flaunt his pride.

Or would a shorter line be better, something utterly simple and heartfelt, limpid tears of grief like spring rain dripping off the petals of a flower?

It was odd, Blacker thought, increasing his pace, how difficult he found writing nature poetry; nature was beautiful, maybe, but it was not stimulating. And it was nature poetry that *Field and Garden* wanted. Still, that pheasant ought to be worth five guineas. *Tread lightly past, Where he lies still, And something last . . .*

11

# THE GREEN FLASH

Damn! In his absorption he had nearly trodden on an-other pheasant. What was happening to the birds? Blacker, who objected to occurrences with no visible explanation, walked on frowning. The path bore downhill to the right, and leaving the hazel grove, crossed a tiny valley. Below him Blacker was surprised to see a small, secretive flint cottage, surrounded on three sides by trees. In front of it was a patch of turf. A deck chair stood there, and a man was peacefully stretched out in it, enjoying the afternoon sun.

Blacker's first impulse was to turn back; he felt as if he had walked into somebody's garden and was filled with mild irritation at the unexpectedness of the encounter; there ought to have been some warning signs, dash it all. The wood had seemed as deserted as Eden itself. But his turning around would have an appearance of guilt and furtiveness; on second thought he decided to go boldly past the cottage. After all there was no fence, and the path was not marked private in any way; he had a perfect right to be there.

"Good afternoon," said the man pleasantly as Blacker approached. "Remarkably fine weather, is it not?"

"I do hope I'm not trespassing."

Studying the man, Blacker revised his first guess. This was no gamekeeper; there was distinction in every line of the thin, sculptured face. What most attracted Blacker's attention were the hands, holding a small gilt coffee cup; they were as white, frail, and attenuated as the pale roots of water plants.

"Not at all," the man said cordially. "In fact you arrive at a most opportune moment; you are very welcome. I was just wishing for a little company. Delightful as I find this sylvan retreat, it becomes, all of a sudden, a little *dull*, a little *banal*. I do trust that you have time to sit down and share my after-lunch coffee and liqueur."

12

As he spoke he reached behind him and brought out a second deck chair from the cottage porch.

"Why, thank you; I should be delighted," said Blacker, wondering if he had the strength of character to take out the ham sandwich and eat it in front of this patrician hermit.

Before he made up his mind the man had gone into the house and returned with another gilt cup full of black, fragrant coffee, hot as Tartarus, which he handed to Blacker. He carried also a tiny glass, and into this, from a blackcurrant cordial bottle, he carefully poured a clear, colorless liquor. Blacker sniffed his glassful with caution, mistrusting the bottle and its evidence of home brewing, but the scent, aromatic and powerful, was similar to that of curaçao, and the liquid moved in its glass with an oily smoothness. It certainly was not cowslip wine.

"Well," said his host, reseating himself and gesturing slightly with his glass, "to your health!" He sipped delicately.

"Cheers," said Blacker, and added, "My name's Roger Blacker." It sounded a little lame. The liqueur was not curaçao, but akin to it, and quite remarkably potent; Blacker, who was very hungry, felt the fumes rise up inside his head as if an orange tree had taken root there and was putting out leaves and golden glowing fruit.

"Sir Francis Deeking," the other man said, and then Blacker understood why his hands had seemed so spectacular, so portentously out of the common.

"The surgeon? But surely you don't live down here?"

Deeking waved a hand deprecatingly. "A weekend retreat. A hermitage, to which I can retire from the strain of my calling."

"It certainly is very remote," Blacker remarked. "It must be five miles from the nearest road."

"Six. And you, my dear Mr. Blacker, what is your profession?"

"Oh, a writer," said Blacker modestly. The drink was having its usual effect on him; he managed to convey not that he was a journalist on a twopenny daily with literary yearnings, but that he was a philosopher and essayist of rare quality, a sort of second Bacon. All the time he spoke, while drawn out most flatteringly by the questions of Sir Francis, he was recalling journalistic scraps of information about his host: the operation on the Indian Prince; the Cabinet Minister's appendix; the amputation performed on that unfortunate ballerina who had both feet crushed in a railway accident; the major operation which had proved so miraculously successful on the American heiress.

"You must feel like a god," he said suddenly, noticing with surprise that his glass was empty. Sir Francis waved the remark aside.

"We all have our godlike attributes," he said, leaning forward. "Now you, Mr. Blacker, a writer, a creative artist—do you not know a power akin to godhead when you transfer your thought to paper?"

"Well, not exactly then," said Blacker, feeling the liqueur moving inside his head in golden and russet-colored clouds. "Not so much then, but I do have one unusual power, a power not shared by many people, of foretelling the future. For instance, as I was coming through the wood, I knew this house would be here. I knew I should find you sitting in front of it. I can look at the list of runners in a race, and the name of the winner fairly leaps out at me from the page, as if it was printed in golden ink. Forthcoming events—air disasters, train crashes—I always sense in advance. I begin to have a terrible feeling of impending doom, as if my brain was a volcano just on the point of eruption."

What was that other item of news about Sir Francis Deeking, he wondered, a recent report, a tiny paragraph that had caught his eye in *The Times*? He could not recall it.

"*Really?*" Sir Francis was looking at him with the keenest interest; his eyes, hooded and fanatical under their heavy lids, held brilliant points of light. "I have always longed to know somebody with such a power. It must be a terrifying responsibility."

"Oh, it is," Blacker said. He contrived to look bowed under the weight of supernatural cares; noticed that his glass was full again, and drained it. "Of course I don't use the faculty for my own ends; something fundamental in me rises up to prevent that. It's as basic, you know, as the instinct forbidding cannibalism or incest—"

"Quite, quite," Sir Francis agreed. "But for another person you would be able to give warnings, advise profitable courses of action—? My dear fellow, your glass is empty. Allow me."

"This is marvelous stuff," Blacker said hazily. "It's like a wreath of orange blossom." He gestured with his finger.

"I distill it myself, from marmalade. But do go on with what you were saying. Could you, for instance, tell me the winner of this afternoon's Manchester Plate?"

"Bow Bells," Blacker said unhesitatingly. It was the only name he could remember.

"You interest me enormously. And the result of today's Aldwych by-election? Do you know that?"

"Unwin, the Liberal, will get in by a majority of two hundred and eighty-two. He won't take his seat, though. He'll

be killed at seven this evening in a lift accident at his hotel."
Blacker was well away by now.

"Will he, indeed?" Sir Francis appeared delighted. "A
pestilent fellow. I have sat on several boards with him. Do
continue."

Blacker required little encouragement. He told the story
of the financier whom he had warned in time of the oil company crash; the dream about the famous violinist which had re-
sulted in the man's canceling his passage on the ill-fated *Orion*;
and the tragic tale of the bullfighter who had ignored his warning.

"But I'm talking too much about myself," he said at
length, partly because he noticed an ominous clogging of his
tongue, a refusal of his thoughts to marshal themselves. He cast
about for an impersonal topic, something simple.

"The pheasants," he said. "What's happened to the
pheasants? Cut down in their prime. It—it's terrible. I found
four in the wood up there, four or five."

"Really?" Sir Francis seemed callously uninterested in
the fate of the pheasants. "It's the chemical sprays they use on
the crops, I understand. Bound to upset the ecology; they
never work out the probable results beforehand. Now if you
were in charge, my dear Mr. Blacker—but forgive me, it is a hot
afternoon and you must be tired and footsore if you have
walked from Witherstow this morning—let me suggest that you
have a short sleep . . ."

His voice seemed to come from farther and farther away;
a network of sun-colored leaves laced themselves in front of
Blacker's eyes. Gratefully he leaned back and stretched out his
aching feet.

Some time after this Blacker roused a little—or was it

only a dream?—to see Sir Francis standing by him, rubbing his hands, with a face of jubilation.

"My dear fellow, my dear Mr. Blacker, what a *lusus naturae* you are. I can never be sufficiently grateful that you came my way. Bow Bells walked home—positively *ambled*. I have been listening to the commentary. What a misfortune that I had no time to place money on the horse—but never mind, never mind, that can be remedied another time.

"It is unkind of me to disturb your well-earned rest, though; drink this last thimbleful and finish your nap while the sun is on the wood."

As Blacker's head sank back against the deck chair again, Sir Francis leaned forward and gently took the glass from his hand.

Sweet river of dreams, thought Blacker, fancy the horse actually winning. I wish I'd had a fiver on it myself; I could do with a new pair of shoes. I should have undone these before I dozed off, they're too tight or something. I must wake up soon, ought to be on my way in half an hour or so . . .

When Blacker finally woke he found that he was lying on a narrow bed, indoors, covered with a couple of blankets. His head ached and throbbed with a shattering intensity, and it took a few minutes for his vision to clear; then he saw that he was in a small white cell-like room, which contained nothing but the bed he was on and a chair. It was very nearly dark.

He tried to struggle up but a strange numbness and heaviness had invaded the lower part of his body, and after hoisting himself onto his elbow he felt so sick that he abandoned the effort and lay down again.

That stuff must have the effect of a knockout drop, he

thought ruefully; what a fool I was to drink it. I'll have to apologize to Sir Francis. What time can it be?

Brisk light footsteps approached the door, and Sir Francis came in. He was carrying a portable radio which he placed on the window sill.

"Ah, my dear Blacker, I see you have come around. Allow me to offer you a drink."

He raised Blacker skillfully, and gave him a drink of water from a cup with a rim and a spout.

"Now let me settle you down again. Excellent. We shall soon have you—well, not on your feet, but sitting up and taking nourishment." He laughed a little. "You can have some beef tea presently."

"I am so sorry," Blacker said. "I really need not trespass on your hospitality any longer. I shall be quite all right in a minute."

"No trespass, my dear friend. You are not at all in the way. I hope that you will be here for a long and pleasant stay. These surroundings, so restful, so conducive to a writer's inspiration—what could be more suitable for you? You need not think that I shall disturb you. I am in London all week, but shall keep you company at weekends—pray, pray don't think that you will be a nuisance or de trop. On the contrary, I am hoping that you can do me the kindness of giving me the Stock Exchange prices in advance, which will amply compensate for any small trouble I have taken. No, no, you must feel quite at home—please consider, indeed, that this is your home."

Stock Exchange prices? It took Blacker a moment to remember, then he thought, Oh lord, my tongue has played me false as usual. He tried to recall what stupidities he had been guilty of. "Those stories," he said lamely, "they were all a bit exaggerated, you know. About my foretelling the future. I can't

18

really. That horse's winning was a pure coincidence, I'm afraid."

"Modesty, modesty." Sir Francis was smiling, but he had gone rather pale, and Blacker noticed a beading of sweat along his cheekbones. "I am sure you will be invaluable. Since my retirement I find it absolutely necessary to augment my income by judicious investment."

All of a sudden Blacker remembered the gist of that small paragraph in *The Times*. Nervous breakdown. Complete rest. Retirement.

"I—I really must go now," he said uneasily, trying to push himself upright. "I meant to be back in town by seven."

"Oh, but Mr. Blacker, that is quite out of the question. Indeed, so as to preclude any such action, I have amputated your feet. But you need not worry; I know you will be very happy here. And I feel certain that you are wrong to doubt your own powers. Let us listen to the nine o'clock news in order to be quite satisfied that the detestable Unwin did fall down the hotel lift shaft."

He walked over to the portable radio and switched it on.

# Sonata for Harp and Bicycle

"No one is *allowed*
to remain in the building after five o'clock," Mr. Manaby told
his new assistant, showing him into the little room that was
like the inside of a parcel.

"Why not?"

"Directorial policy," said Mr. Manaby. But that was
not the real reason.

Gaunt and sooty, Grimes Buildings lurched up the
side of a hill toward Clerkenwell. Every little office within its
dim and crumbling exterior owned one tiny crumb of light—
such was the proud boast of the architect—but toward evening
the crumbs were collected as by an immense vacuum cleaner,

absorbed and demolished, yielding to an uncontrollable mass of dark that came tumbling in through windows and doors to take their place. Darkness infested the building like a flight of bats returning willingly to roost.

"Wash hands, please. Wash hands, please," the intercom began to bawl in the passages at a quarter to five. Without much need of prompting, the staff hustled like lemmings along the corridors to green- and blue-tiled washrooms that mocked with an illusion of cheerfulness the encroaching dusk.

"All papers into cases, please," the voice warned, five minutes later. "Look at your desks, ladies and gentlemen. Any documents left lying about? Kindly put them away. Desks must be left clear and tidy. Drawers must be shut."

A multitudinous shuffling, a rustling as of innumerable bluebottle flies might have been heard by the attentive ear after this injunction, as the employees of Moreton Wold and Company thrust their papers into cases, hurried letters and invoices into drawers, clipped statistical abstracts together and slammed them into filing cabinets, dropped discarded copy into wastepaper baskets. Two minutes later, and not a desk throughout Grimes Buildings bore more than its customary coating of dust.

"Hats and coats on, please. Hats and coats on, please. Did you bring an umbrella? Have you left any shopping on the floor?" At three minutes to five the homegoing throng was in the lifts and on the stairs; a clattering, staccato-voiced flood darkened momentarily the great double doors of the building, and then as the first faint notes of St. Paul's came echoing faintly on the frosty air, to be picked up near at hand by the louder chimes of St. Biddulph's-on-the-Wall, the entire premises of Moreton Wold stood empty.

"But why is it?" Jason Ashgrove, the new copywriter, asked his secretary one day. "Why are the staff herded out so

21

fast? Not that I'm against it, mind you; I think it's an admirable idea in many ways, but there is the liberty of the individual to be considered, don't you think?"

"Hush!" Miss Golden, the secretary, gazed at him with large and terrified eyes. "You mustn't ask that sort of question. When you are taken onto the Established Staff you'll be told. Not before."

"But I want to know *now*," Jason said in discontent. "Do you know?"

"Yes, I do," Miss Golden answered tantalizingly. "Come on, or we shan't have finished the Oat Crisp layout by a quarter to." And she stared firmly down at the copy in front of her, lips folded, candyfloss hair falling over her face, lashes hiding eyes like peridots, a girl with a secret.

Jason was annoyed. He rapped out a couple of rude and witty rhymes which Miss Golden let pass in a withering silence.

"What do you want for your birthday, Miss Golden? Sherry? Fudge? Bubble bath?"

"I want to go away with a clear conscience about Oat Crisps," Miss Golden retorted. It was not true; what she chiefly wanted was Mr. Jason Ashgrove, but he had not realized this yet.

"Come on, don't tease! I'm sure you haven't been on the Established Staff all that long," he coaxed her. "What happens when one is taken on, anyway? Does the Managing Director have us up for a confidential chat? Or are we given a little book called *The Awful Secret of Grimes Buildings?*"

Miss Golden wasn't telling. She opened her drawer and took out a white towel and a cake of rosy soap.

"Wash hands, please! Wash hands, please!"

## Sonata for Harp and Bicycle

Jason was frustrated. "You'll be sorry," he said. "I shall do something desperate."

"Oh no, you mustn't!" Her eyes were large with fright. She ran from the room and was back within a couple of moments, still drying her hands.

"If I took you out for a coffee, couldn't you give me just a tiny hint?"

Side by side Miss Golden and Mr. Ashgrove ran along the green-floored passages, battled down the white marble stairs among the hundred other employees from the tenth floor, the nine hundred from the floors below.

He saw her lips move as she said something, but in the clatter of two thousand feet the words were lost.

"—fire escape," he heard, as they came into the momentary hush of the carpeted entrance hall. And "—it's to do with a bicycle. A bicycle and a harp."

"I don't understand."

Now they were in the street, chilly with the winter dusk smells of celery on carts, of swept-up leaves heaped in faraway parks, and cold layers of dew sinking among the withered evening primroses in the bombed areas. London lay about them wreathed in twilit mystery and fading against the barred and smoky sky. Like a ninth wave the sound of traffic overtook and swallowed them.

"Please tell me!"

But, shaking her head, she stepped onto a scarlet homebound bus and was borne away from him.

Jason stood undecided on the pavement, with the crowds dividing around him as around the pier of a bridge. He scratched his head, looked about him for guidance.

An ambulance clanged, a taxi hooted, a drill stuttered, a

23

siren wailed on the river, a door slammed, a brake squealed, and close beside his ear a bicycle bell tinkled its tiny warning.

A bicycle, she had said. A bicycle and a harp.

Jason turned and stared at Grimes Buildings.

Somewhere, he knew, there was a back way in, a service entrance. He walked slowly past the main doors, with their tubs of snowy chrysanthemums, and up Glass Street. A tiny furtive wedge of darkness beckoned him, a snicket, a hacket, an alley carved into the thickness of the building. It was so narrow that at any moment, it seemed, the overtopping walls would come together and squeeze it out of existence.

Walking as softly as an Indian, Jason passed through it, slid by a file of dustbins, and found the foot of the fire escape. Iron treads rose into the mist, like an illustration to a Gothic fairy tale.

He began to climb.

When he had mounted to the ninth story he paused for breath. It was a lonely place. The lighting consisted of a dim bulb at the foot of every flight. A well of gloom sank beneath him. The cold fingers of the wind nagged and fluttered at the tails of his jacket, and he pulled the string of the fire door and edged inside.

Grimes Buildings were triangular, with the street forming the base of the triangle, and the fire escape the point. Jason could see two long passages coming toward him, meeting at an acute angle where he stood. He started down the left-hand one, tiptoeing in the cavelike silence. Nowhere was there any sound, except for the faraway drip of a tap. No night watchman would stay in the building; none was needed. Burglars gave the place a wide berth.

Jason opened a door at random; then another. Offices

lay everywhere about him, empty and forbidding. Some held lipstick-stained tissues, spilled powder, and orange peels; others were still foggy with cigarette smoke. Here was a Director's suite of rooms—a desk like half an acre of frozen lake, inch-thick carpet, roses, and the smell of cigars. Here was a conference room with scattered squares of doodled blotting paper. All equally empty.

He was not sure when he first began to notice the bell. Telephone, he thought at first, and then he remembered that all the outside lines were disconnected at five. And this bell, anyway, had not the regularity of a telephone's double ring: there was a tinkle, and then silence; a long ring, and then silence; a whole volley of rings together, and then silence.

Jason stood listening, and fear knocked against his ribs and shortened his breath. He knew that he must move or be paralyzed by it. He ran up a flight of stairs and found himself with two more endless green corridors beckoning him like a pair of dividers.

Another sound now: a waft of ice-thin notes, riffling up an arpeggio like a flurry of snowflakes. Far away down the passage it echoed. Jason ran in pursuit, but as he ran the music receded. He circled the building, but it always outdistanced him, and when he came back to the stairs he heard it fading away to the story below.

He hesitated, and as he did so heard again the bell; the bicycle bell. It was approaching him fast, bearing down on him, urgent, menacing. He could hear the pedals, almost see the shimmer of an invisible wheel. Absurdly, he was reminded of the insistent clamor of an ice-cream vendor, summoning children on a sultry Sunday afternoon.

There was a little fireman's alcove beside him, with buckets and pumps. He hurled himself into it. The bell stopped beside him, and then there was a moment while his heart tried to shake itself loose in his chest. He was looking into two eyes carved out of expressionless air; he was held by two hands knotted together out of the width of dark.

"Daisy, Daisy?" came the whisper. "Is that you, Daisy? Have you come to give me your answer?"

Jason tried to speak, but no words came.

"It's not Daisy! Who are you?" The sibilants were full of threat. "You can't stay here. This is private property."

He was thrust along the corridor. It was like being pushed by a whirlwind—the fire door opened ahead of him without a touch, and he was on the openwork platform, clutching the slender railing. Still the hands would not let him go.

"How about it?" the whisper mocked him. "How about jumping? It's an easy death compared with some."

Jason looked down into the smoky void. The darkness nodded to him like a familiar.

"You wouldn't be much loss, would you? What have you got to live for?"

Miss Golden, Jason thought. She would miss me. And the syllables Berenice Golden lingered in the air like a chime. Drawing on some unknown deposit of courage he shook himself loose from the holding hands and ran down the fire escape without looking back.

Next morning when Miss Golden, crisp, fragrant, and punctual, shut the door of Room 492 behind her, she stopped short of the hat-pegs with a horrified gasp.

"Mr. Ashgrove, your hair!"

"It makes me look more distinguished, don't you think?" he said.

It had indeed this effect, for his impeccable dark cut had

turned to a stippled silver which might have been envied by many a diplomat.

"How did it happen? You've not—" her voice sank to a whisper—"you've not been in Grimes Buildings after dark?"

"Miss Golden—Berenice," he said earnestly. "Who was Daisy? Plainly you know. Tell me the story."

"Did you see him?" she asked faintly.

"Him?"

"William Heron—The Wailing Watchman. Oh," she exclaimed in terror, "I can see you did. Then you are doomed —doomed!"

"If I'm doomed," said Jason, "let's have coffee, and you tell me the story quickly."

"It all happened over fifty years ago," said Berenice, as she spooned out coffee powder with distracted extravagance. "Heron was the night watchman in this building, patrolling the corridors from dusk to dawn every night on his bicycle. He fell in love with a Miss Bell who taught the harp. She rented a room—this room—and gave lessons in it. She began to reciprocate his love, and they used to share a picnic supper every night at eleven, and she'd stay on a while to keep him company. It was an idyll, among the fire buckets and the furnace pipes.

"On Halloween he had summoned up the courage to propose to her. The day before he had told her he was going to ask her a very important question, and he came to the Buildings with a huge bunch of roses and a bottle of wine. But Miss Bell never turned up.

"The explanation was simple. Miss Bell, of course, had been losing a lot of sleep through her nocturnal romance, and so she used to take a nap in her music room between seven and ten, to save going home. In order to make sure that she would wake up, she persuaded her father, a distant relative of Graham

Bell, to attach an alarm-waking fixture to her telephone which called her every night at ten. She was too modest and shy to let Heron know that she spent those hours in the building, and to give him the pleasure of waking her himself.

"Alas! On this important evening the line failed, and she never woke up. The telephone was in its infancy at that time, you must remember.

"Heron waited and waited. At last, mad with grief and jealousy, having called her home and discovered that she was not there, he concluded that she had betrayed him; he ran to the fire escape, and cast himself off it, holding the roses and the bottle of wine.

"Daisy did not long survive him but pined away soon after. Since that day their ghosts have haunted Grimes Buildings, he vainly patrolling the corridors on his bicycle, she playing her harp in the room she rented. But they never meet. And anyone who meets the ghost of William Heron will himself, within five days, leap down from the same fatal fire escape."

She gazed at him with tragic eyes.

"In that case we must lose no time," said Jason, and he enveloped her in an embrace as prompt as it was ardent. Looking down at the gossamer hair sprayed across his pin-stripe, he added, "Just the same it is a preposterous situation. Firstly, I have no intention of jumping off the fire escape—" here, however, he repressed a shudder as he remembered the cold, clutching hands of the evening before—"and secondly, I find it quite nonsensical that those two inefficient ghosts have spent fifty years in this building without coming across each other. We must remedy the matter, Berenice. We must not begrudge our new-found happiness to others."

He gave her another kiss so impassioned that the electric typewriter against which they were leaning began chattering to itself in a frenzy of enthusiasm.

"This very evening," he went on, looking at his watch, "we will put matters right for that unhappy couple and then, if I really have only five more days to live, which I don't for one moment believe, we will proceed to spend them together, my bewitching Berenice, in the most advantageous manner possible."

She nodded, spellbound.

"Can you work a switchboard?" he added. She nodded again. "My love, you are perfection itself. Meet me in the switchboard room then, at ten this evening. I would say, have dinner with me, but I shall need to make one or two purchases and see an old R.A.F. friend. You will be safe from Heron's curse in the switchboard room if he always keeps to the corridors."

"I would rather meet him and die with you," she murmured.

"My angel, I hope that won't be necessary. Now," he said, sighing, "I suppose we should get down to our day's work."

Strangely enough the copy they wrote that day, although engendered from such agitated minds, sold more packets of Oat Crisps than any other advertising matter before or since.

That evening when Jason entered Grimes Buildings he was carrying two bottles of wine, two bunches of red roses, and a large canvas-covered bundle. Miss Golden, who had concealed herself in the switchboard room before the offices closed for the night, eyed these things with surprise.

"Now," said Jason, after he had greeted her, "I want you first to ring our own extension."

"No one will reply, surely?"

"I think *she* will reply."

Sure enough, when Berenice rang Extension 170 a faint, sleepy voice, distant and yet clear, whispered, "Hullo?"

"Is that Miss Bell?"

"Yes."

Berenice went a little pale. Her eyes sought Jason's and, prompted by him, she said formally, "Switchboard here, Miss Bell. Your ten o'clock call."

"Thank you," the faint voice said. There was a click and the line went blank.

"Excellent," Jason remarked. He unfastened his package and slipped its straps over his shoulders. "Now plug into the intercom."

Berenice did so, and then said, loudly and clearly, "Attention. Night watchman on duty, please. Night watchman on duty. You have an urgent summons to Room 492. You have an urgent summons to Room 492." The intercom echoed and reverberated through the empty corridors, then coughed itself to silence.

"Now we must run. You take the roses, sweetheart, and I'll carry the bottles."

Together they raced up eight flights of stairs and along the passages to Room 492. As they neared the door a burst of music met them—harp music swelling out, sweet and triumphant. Jason took a bunch of roses from Berenice, opened the door a little way, and gently deposited them, with a bottle, inside the door. As he closed it again Berenice said breathlessly, "Did you see anyone?"

30

"No," he said. "The room was too full of music." She saw that his eyes were shining.

They stood hand in hand, reluctant to move away, waiting for they hardly knew what. Suddenly the door opened again. Neither Berenice nor Jason, afterward, would speak of what they saw but each was left with a memory, bright as the picture on a Salvador Dali calendar, of a bicycle bearing on its saddle a harp, a bottle of wine, and a bouquet of red roses, sweeping improbably down the corridor and far, far away.

"We can go now," Jason said.

He led Berenice to the fire door, tucking the bottle of Médoc in his jacket pocket. A black wind from the north whistled beneath them as they stood on the openwork platform, looking down.

"We don't want our evening to be spoiled by the thought of a curse hanging over us," he said, "so this is the practical thing to do. Hang onto the roses." And holding his love firmly, Jason pulled the rip cord of his R.A.F. friend's parachute and leaped off the fire escape.

A bridal shower of rose petals adorned the descent of Miss Golden, who was possibly the only girl to be kissed in midair in the district of Clerkenwell at ten minutes to midnight on Halloween.

31

# The Dreamers

Mr. Bodkin sat over his breakfast in a trance of thought so deep, so prolonged, that, if the blood does indeed rise into the head and assist mental processes, porridge, kidneys and coffee, it must be assumed, were not so much digested as assimilated in a whirlpool of thought.

Mrs. Bodkin, his charming wife, looked at him over the coffeepot but made no attempt to break into his meditations. Her husband, from time to time, gave her a kindly though absent glance, and from this she drew her own conclusions. These were in some degree correct, for he was considering the choice of a present for her birthday.

32

## The Dreamers

Should it be the pressure cooker or the electric bed-warmer? He had inclined toward the bedwarmer at first, as he shivered in the chilly dining room. His dear Hieratica never remembered to switch on the fire sufficiently early; he had mentioned it several times and then resigned himself to cold passivity. But, as the porridge went down in rasping chunks, he began to consider the virtues of pressure cookers; they made, he had heard, admirable porridge, and then they were so economical—which would be sure to appeal to Hieratica. Since the money they lived on was hers, he found it harder to criticize her economies than her porridge.

If he bought the warmer, he could use it when Hieratica no longer required it; but then a pressure cooker would be useful too; it was impossible to decide. He opened his mouth to speak, but at that moment Hieratica remembered something, and cried:

"There! I never told you my dream."

Mr. Bodkin sighed. As they had dressed, he had observed the portentous but joyful expression on his wife's face which showed that she had had another of her dreams. The very way in which she had buckled her watchstrap and tied her shoelaces gave the same evidence. These dreams were becoming more and more frequent, and occupied a larger and larger part of the domestic scene.

"I dreamed that I was the wife of an international financier," she announced.

"Yes, dear."

"He was a Mohammedan, and I was his fourth wife—the youngest, and much the most beautiful. He was rather old, I remember, and the other wives were all jealous of me because I was the favorite."

"Naturally."

"Well. I was going with him to a currency conference in Athens, and we had to cross the mountains. We were waylaid, and he was murdered by his unscrupulous enemies, and they dragged his body to a cave. I watched over it—they hadn't touched me—till I was found, two days later, and then he was taken down to Athens, and there was a grand funeral for him. I had no mourning clothes, so I had to walk behind the coffin in a black silk petticoat. Imagine it!"

"Yes indeed."

"A young man saw me from a balcony, and fell madly in love with me. Three weeks later we were married."

"Is that all?"

"I *think* there's some more," she said, frowning and concentrating. "It may come back to me. I was madly beautiful, I do know, and the young man—his name was Alexis—was terribly handsome."

"It must have been very nice. If you have a moment to spare, I was going to ask you about your birthday present. Would you prefer an electric bedwarmer, or a pressure cooker?"

"Oh Thomas! You kind, thoughtful creature! Gracious now, which would I rather have?"

In trying to decide, she remembered some more of her dream, which had to be told.

"About your present," he began again, as they left the table. "You really must choose—I've decided to leave your fate in your own hands." He smiled at her.

"There, I never did, did I? Isn't it difficult? Would you think me terribly greedy if I had both?"

"I should go on thinking of you," said Thomas politely, "in exactly the same way."

The warmer *and* the cooker—that was certainly a simple

## The Dreamers

solution, and as the money would come out of their joint account the cost did not matter. There was plenty in it.

"I'll be home at lunch time, I expect, my dear."

He strolled off into the town, thinking about Hieratica and her dreams. He was a good-natured creature, easily pleased. Given a moderate degree of comfort and an assured future, he could be complacent about his wife's occasional playful epithets of "parasite" and "loafer." He had no real anxieties, and these things were hardly more than pleasant sharpnesses—little drops of vinegar to break up the oil of his smooth existence.

But the dreams, which were becoming longer and longer, more and more frequent, seemed to him a vague threat; his placid mind was a little troubled by them. Hieratica, he knew, liked to be annoying, and long, boring recitals were merely the development of a new technique framed for this purpose. He was not worried on that score. His own thought processes were so satisfactory that he was able, at any moment, to absent his mind from her conversation.

What caused his disquiet was the undisguised romance, the wishful quality which her dreams were acquiring. It would not be long, he reasoned, before she began to demand from waking life this Arabian Nights flavor—a flavor which he neither intended, nor was able, to create. What would Hieratica do then? She was an energetic woman. She might elect for a Mediterranean cruise, disagreeable thought. She might even contemplate divorce. He suspected she knew, or that she suspected, activities of his which would make this a possibility.

He felt fairly certain, however, that she had not yet begun to equate her dreams with her real experiences. If the dreams could be stopped in time, there was a good chance of calamity being averted.

# THE GREEN FLASH

The windows of a big store gleamed at him across the pavement, and he stepped inside and began to make inquiries.

Thomas was late for lunch—so late that Hieratica put the dishes into the oven, and retiring to the sitting room sank into a waking dream—not one of the romances which illuminated her nights, but a dream of a more practical nature. Suppose Thomas, she mused, were now visiting a heart specialist? She had noticed that he was somewhat anxious and preoccupied lately, seemed pale, seemed flushed. Perhaps he suspected some deep-seated malady, impossible to eradicate? He was now, perhaps, hearing the confirmation of this from a grave, keen-eyed doctor, who would not spare him the distressing details. Thomas had tidied his desk on Thursday—surely that portended something unusual? He had given up trying not to smoke, as if it were not worth the effort in the short time that remained to him. He had been hurrying to finish War and Peace, but had declared that he would not begin Anna Karenina. It all pointed in the same direction.

Hieratica was mildly pleased at her fancy. She hated the thought of a divorce, with all its fuss and publicity. She would be a handsome and wealthy widow, free to set out perhaps on a cruise to Egypt or Greece. There was a charming black hat in Suzanne's window—it might be a good plan to go and buy it on Monday, a black hat was always useful. Then there were the announcements in the papers to think of, and the letters to friends. She was rising to find a pencil when she heard the sound of Thomas's latch-key. He came in carrying a box, in which reposed a heavy gleaming sphere as large as a small milk churn: the pressure cooker.

"The warmer won't be here till Monday," he explained. "They hadn't the single bed size in stock. I brought the cooker with me. You can cook a whole dinner in thirty minutes, and they say it will reduce bones to jelly in two hours."

Hieratica was suitably delighted, and they went in to lunch chatting agreeably about the uses of this new acquisition.

During the afternoon she had a nap, and thus, at six-thirty, just as the opening bars of his favorite violin concerto came from the wireless, gay and formal as a Christmas tree, she was able to tell Thomas every detail of her latest dream. She had been trapped at the top of a lift shaft, doomed, if she had not been lowered to safety on a long rope by the handsome elevator attendant.

By Monday's parcel post came the electric bedwarmer.

"I'll fix that faulty power point in our room before tonight," said Thomas. Hieratica was pleased at the unusual devotion with which he tinkered upstairs for a couple of hours. It might be conscience-work, hastily performed before death stepped in and made it too late.

"I think you'll find it's working satisfactorily now," he said, as she got into bed that night, after re-trying the new hat. "I'll switch it on, shall I? Have you got your feet on it?"

He pressed the switch and watched benignly as Hieratica, with the slightest quiver, slipped into a long and dreamless sleep.

"I must write to the makers and congratulate them," he thought.

He also wrote to the manufacturers of the pressure cooker to tell them that their product more than fulfilled its promise and had given him every satisfaction.

Later that summer a neighbor called out a greeting to Thomas, leisurely at work in his garden, and asked when Mrs. Bodkin was expected back from her long tour of the Middle East.

"Her return has been indefinitely postponed," Thomas answered. "She finds her present existence most congenial. I expect to be on my own for a long time."

The neighbor nodded sympathetically.

"Marvelous show of roses you have this summer," he commented. "How do you do it?"

"Bone manure," Thomas replied. "Bone manure."

# Follow My Fancy

"Uranium," said the captain. "Uranium 235." The words glittered on his tongue like sparks from a gold-filled tooth.

There was no crew. The only answer came from the wind, which sang in the rigging of his crazy old ship like the music of Orpheus. Jake Brandywine looked about him thoughtfully. The decks were clear. The sails were stowed, since there would be no need for them. Insofar as was possible, old Argo was trim and ready for the voyage.

Provisions? He had laid in a thousand breakfast biscuits, a thousand tins of lunch meat, a thousand tea cakes, a thousand bottles of dinner wine; food for over three years. And if, despite this store, hunger gnawed at him like an old rat, he could munch away at his supply of charcoal, brought for sketching seascapes.

Nevertheless, the captain had a hunted, haunted look in his eye; he glanced continually about him, started at sounds, and grabbed convulsively at the mast ropes when sea-swallows swooped past. His hand, holding the little soapstone box of uranium shook uncontrollably, white at the knuckles, and sweat darted glistening on his forehead. He had the air of a man pursued by the furies, escaping only just in time.

To learn the reason for this state of affairs we must go back some months, and shift our scene to the luxuriously appointed consulting room of a Harley Street psychiatrist.

Dr. Killgruel looked at his patient appraisingly, noted the fine-drawn lines around eyes and mouth, the restless movements, the unsteady hands.

"You are Jake Brandywine the artist?" he inquired.

The patient nodded.

"I admire your work," said the doctor. "I am the possessor of an early Brandywine myself." He flicked a speck from his snowy sleeve. "Now, what is your trouble precisely?"

Jake looked somewhat shamefaced.

"You need not be embarrassed," said the doctor. "I can see that you are suffering from nervous exhaustion, a state which leads people into all sorts of odd activities, of no importance in themselves. One of my patients, for instance, suffers from a compulsion to get up in the night and eat the cheese out of the mousetraps in the pantry. His fingers are terribly badly bruised, and he has chronic indigestion. But I interrupt."

He placed his fingertips together and looked attentively at Jake.

"My trouble is not like that exactly," Jake said. "It undoubtedly began with exhaustion. There is, as perhaps you know, an enormous demand for my work at present, not only by private buyers, but also for tube stations, corner-houses, town halls, piers, and public lavatories. About a month ago I had been rushing to finish a series of murals for restaurant cars, working nineteen and twenty hours a day, and was suffering from acute physical fatigue. I live some distance from the center of London, on the 93 bus route, and just at this time the service had been cut; I used to work all night and go home in the middle of the day, and in my exhausted state it seemed to me that I spent my entire life either working or waiting for buses that failed to appear.

"Well, one day, to pass the time, I started willing the bus to come; I imagined it cruising past Woolworths, along to the Town Hall, around the corner, over the railway bridge, and down to the bus stop. When I stopped concentrating and looked up, there was a 93, sure enough. Of course I was amused, and thought it nothing but a coincidence, but the next day the same thing happened, and every day after that; it became a sort of game which I played to distract myself."

The doctor nodded.

"That was all right. I didn't really take it seriously, you understand. But one evening when I was literally staggering with fatigue, I was waiting in Oxford Street for a bus to take me to Hyde Park corner, and unconsciously, without intending to, I started playing my game. A flash of red caught my eye, I looked up, and there was a 93—a bus which, as you know, has no right to be in Oxford Street at all."

He stopped and gazed, hollow-eyed, at the doctor, who smiled sympathetically.

"It must have been a dreadful moment," he agreed. "What did you do?"

41

"I took a taxi."

"Very sensible." The doctor's tone was approving. "Take as many as you can while the delusion lasts."

"But Doctor, it was no delusion. It was a real bus. And since then it has happened repeatedly. I can't stop thinking about 93 buses, and they keep turning up everywhere. What terrifies me is the thought that sooner or later I shall fetch one down into the underground or a turkish bath or—or a canoe in the Serpentine—"

"Come, come," said Dr. Killgruel. "These are morbid fears. We can deal with them at once, very easily. Then I'll give you a tonic to set you right. You know quite well that your subconscious won't let you will a bus to appear in an unsuitable place any more than, for example, a hypnotic subject will let himself be ordered to do something which violates his conscience. He just refuses. Now, just to convince you, and make your mind easy on this point, I order you to will a 93 bus into this room."

"No, no!" exclaimed Brandywine, white with terror. "For god's sake, Doctor, don't make me do that!"

Dr. Killgruel was implacable.

"You must put yourself in my hands, or I can do nothing for you. Will the bus to appear—I command you."

Jake gave him a desperate look and then with a visible effort summoned his forces as if he were drawing a deep breath.

There was a rending sound, a frantic tooting, a screech of brakes, and with a last burst of resolution Jake dragged the doctor to one side as a 93 bus bore triumphantly down upon them.

Dr. Killgruel was in hospital for two months. Jake hardly liked to go and see him, since he himself had escaped with bruises and a concussion, though his state of mind was such that the number of 93 buses on London Transport's roster was more than trebled.

But when the doctor came out, he summoned Jake for another consultation.

"Your case interests me," he said. "I've been thinking a lot about it, and I can see that until you're cured, which I'm convinced is only a matter of time, we must effect a transference."

"A transference?"

"Your remarkably powerful will must be trained on some object more suitable than a 93 bus. Can you think of anything else occupying a large part of your attention? There are generally several things of the sort in one's mind such as broken shirt buttons or lost letters."

"My life was so well organized until this business began," said Jake mournfully.

"Are you married?" asked Dr. Killgruel.

Jake shook his head. "I have a char," he said with brevity.

"Is there no female person present in your thoughts?"

At this Jake paused and a shadow came over his face. Then he said slowly, "I suppose you might say that of Miss M."

Pressed to explain himself, he gave an account of Miss M.

He rented his studio from the art department of a fashion magazine called *Fancy*, which had more space than it required in its offices, and where he felt comfortably anonymous among the elegancies of typists and the detached Plymouth Brotherhood of typographers. The arrangement had worked admirably for a year, but recently there had been some internal rearrangements among the personnel of *Fancy*, and he discovered that the editress, Miss Milk, had been installed in the room next to his.

The first intimation he had was a series of melancholy howls which began at half past ten each morning and continued throughout the day. These were explained when he found himself being scrutinized malevolently through the window by a pair of sapphire eyes; Miss M's Siamese was outside on the sill. He opened the window but was so repelled by the neurotic clamor raised by the creature that he shot it out into the passage.

This provoked the first of a series of notes: "Dear Mr. Brandywine, if you let Judas into your room, please see that he is returned to Room 515; he must not be allowed to wander about the building, as he gets lost." It was written on Fancy notepaper, thick as steel plate, in an arrogant black hand, and signed with the initials A.M.

Brandywine resolved that never again should Judas set foot in his room, but it was impossible to adhere to this resolution as spring turned to sweltering summer, and he was obliged to leave the windows open. Judas would come in, patter superciliously around the room, making Jake nervous by long silences and sudden querulous howls; then he would disappear through the window to his owner's room, incurring a perfect torrent of notes from Miss M: could Mr. Brandywine keep his room cleaner; Judas had to be shampooed to get the charcoal dust out of his fur; could Mr. Brandywine put away his paints when not in use as Judas had returned with chrome yellow on his paws and flake white on his tail; would Mr. Brandywine please refrain from feeding Judas (this when he had been driven to the vain resort of sardine sandwiches for pacificatory purposes) as one meal a day was sufficient for any Siamese.

Each note was signed A.M. and the initials began to

have a malignant significance in Jake's mind. He pictured Miss Milk as a sort of embodied capital letter, a black gallows of a woman with square upper-case shoulders and feet like serifs.

"Splendid," said the doctor at the end of this recital. "She will form the nexus of an excellent fixation. You must think about her all you can, and arrange to meet her. Reality is always more useful than imagination. And move up to town, out of range of the 93 buses. Come back and see me in a fortnight."

Next morning Brandywine was in his studio meditating pretexts for meeting Miss M when the telephone rang and a frightened voice twittered into his ear that Miss Milk would be pleased if he would step around and have coffee with her at eleven-three. His state of mind hovered between alarm and elation at this rapid development; the transference seemed to be taking place with disconcerting speed.

When he entered Miss M's room he found her sitting in an attitude that would have been inelegant in most women; she was tipped back in her chair, crossed ankles resting on the corner of her desk. But all Brandywine could think was that she resembled a swallow, with the bird's slender, elongated silhouette. She was wearing a close-fitting, dark, smoke-blue dress, which heightened the impression; wings of black hair, faintly silvered, were brushed back above haughty blue eyes and an angular profile.

She nodded coldly at Brandywine, indicating a chair, and a terrified little secretary scurried forward with a cup of coffee. Jake felt that unless he asserted himself now he was lost. "I wonder if you could let me have a drop of cognac," he said hoarsely. "I find I can't get through the day unless I have one at this time."

When he returned to his studio an hour later his mind

was in a ferment. Miss M had commissioned a series of illustrations for *Fancy* at less than a third of his usual price, and she had also said that they must have lunch on Tuesday, a drink on Wednesday, and dinner on Thursday.

"What was the other thing I had to do?" he wondered, leaning out of his window, and distractedly tearing up little bits of paper. The sight of windows across the road ornamented with swirls of whitewash reminded him; he was supposed to find a flat in town. If that one was empty, he might as well inquire about it.

His hopes were justified, and he moved in without delay, the only proviso from the landlord being that he must not upset the tenant on the top flat, who did not care for dogs, modern music, or late parties.

He arrived home late the following evening to find a note stuck in his letter-box, and stood reading it by the landing light. It said: "Tenant No. 17. Please do not leave fish heads on the fire escape. A.M."

He was still digesting this when a perfumed, dark-blue presence rustled up the stairs to him, closely followed by a Siamese.

A fortnight later Brandywine staggered into Dr. Killgruel's room more dead than alive.

"Well," said the doctor with interest. "How are things going? Are you getting the 93's reduced?"

"93's—" Jake brushed them aside. "It's not them, Doctor, it's Atalanta. She's killing me."

"Who?"

"Atalanta—Miss Milk. I can't sleep, I can't work, I can't think—she's always turning up. At seven in the morning she wants to borrow my spatula, at midnight she drops in saying

46

she's run out of olive oil. Look at me—I've lost twenty pounds already."

"Is she beautiful?" inquired Killgruel professionally.

"Beautiful?" Jake groaned furiously. "My god, Doctor, she's a fiend. You should hear her berating that unfortunate child who works for her, or blowing up at the char, or chiseling some wretched author down to subsistence rates. I shall go crazy. I can't stop thinking about her."

"I'd like to see her."

Jake threw him a look of despair, the door opened, and Miss M sailed in.

"It's good of you to spare me a moment," she said to Killgruel. "It isn't for myself—my health is always excellent, naturally—but Judas has been feeling the heat and seems to be rather nervy."

Poor Jake burst into tears and ran out of the room.

When Killgruel next saw Jake he was surprisingly calm and composed.

"I've made my own plans," he said. "I must get away from everything."

"An excellent plan," agreed the doctor. "Where are you going?"

"I've applied for the job of captain on the *Argo*."

"The *Argo*!" said Killgruel, startled. Recently the papers had been full of the battered old schooner which was going to be the first craft powered solely by uranium. A little piece no bigger than a hazel nut, inserted in a special chamber under the stern would, it was suggested, propel the aged ship forever, like the tiny Japanese boats which dart about saucers of warm water impelled by little bits of camphor.

# THE GREEN FLASH

The only question unsolved was whether *Argo*, once launched, could be made to stop? No anchor cable would hold her; it was possible that a negative reaction might be started to neutralize the force under her keel, but this must be a matter of speculation until the experiment was carried out. There was a chance, therefore, that the man who hazarded himself on her worm-eaten decks was due to be a second Flying Dutchman, borne in a random circle around the earth's circumference forever.

Jake seemed to relish the prospect.

"Frankly, I've had enough of civilization," he said. "A life in which one can be dogged by female fashion editors and 93 buses is no life for me."

"But," Dr. Killgruel objected, "what's to stop them from following you on board?"

"Navigation," Jake answered. "My mind will be too occupied for the first year. I've never been good at mathematics, and I shan't have any attention to spare."

"It will come easier after a while."

"By that time I shall have recovered, or if not," said Jake decisively, "I shall throw myself overboard."

Dr. Killgruel could not entirely approve this course, but he saw that Brandywine's mind was made up.

The press of the world waited in excitement for the launching of *Argo*, but it waited at a distance; Jake had been particular that he should be left alone on the lonely Essex beach that was the taking-off point. Also, and this was perhaps a more cogent reason, there was the possibility of a nuclear explosion when the uranium was first subjected to the activating current.

# Follow My Fancy

Here was Jake, then, pacing about the deck, which sparkled with February frost, and glancing from time to time along the pale deserted line of sand, fringed with a white tidemark. Gulls keened, the wind sang, sharp gusts of sand, "travelers," blew from time to time past *Argo's* keel in an offshore wind as she snuggled deeper and deeper into her bed of sand and ooze.

The shipping lanes had been cleared, helicopters hovered at a respectful distance, and telegrams from statesmen and heads of governments were pinned to the mast; also photographs, sent by enthusiastic schoolgirls.

At length Jake's anxious vigil was at an end; glancing for a last time at his watch, he climbed awkwardly down the swinging rope ladder over the stern, with care deposited the soapstone box and its precious contents in the prepared chamber, and snapped home the protective door. Then he swung himself back on deck, checked the time again, drew a deep breath, and pulled the switch of a tiny battery lying in the forecastle.

There was a convulsive jerk and shudder as *Argo* tore herself loose from the mud, and then, with an unbelievably smooth and lightning-swift motion she darted off, cutting through the choppy sea like a razor.

"We've done it!" Jake cried, his face brilliant with happiness. "I'm free!" And he patted the old ship on her carved wooden quarter-deck railings before swinging himself aft to unlash the rudder and turn her on the agreed course down-Channel.

She was followed in her flight by numerous aircraft. No ship could keep her in view, though many had a brief glimpse of her, masts set back like a scalded cat, scudding through the mist on her way to the South Atlantic.

Radio stations kept track of her progress as she fled by

49

the Argentine coast and rounded Cape Horn; storm or shine meant nothing to her, she was through all weather before it could affect her.

The sole message transmitted by her captain from time to time was, "All well." In two days he had completed his first circuit of the world, in seven the urgently repeated question "Can you stop?" was answered by a laconic "No," and *Argo* pursued her crazy course into infinity.

Scientists, distressed at the thought of Jake skating over the world's aqueous surface for the rest of his life, like a grain of sand on an eyeball, worked night and day at the problem of how to put a brake on *Argo's* career. But no signs of distress came from Jake.

On a summer day some months later Dr. Killgruel was visited by Miss M. They had become friends since the departure of Brandywine, and the visit was nothing unusual, but she was looking pale, he thought, and rather sad; she said she was run down and needed a tonic.

"You hear nothing from Mr. Brandywine, I suppose?" she asked, and he noticed a wistful tone to her voice. "You know, it's odd, but I miss him terribly. I suppose he doesn't even think of me."

For the first time since he had met her she looked human, Killgruel reflected; human and vulnerable. There were tears in her eyes, even.

"I'm tired," she said miserably. "I can't work up any enthusiasm for *Fancy* nowadays. If only I thought he sometimes remembered me it would be a little better."

"Perhaps he will later on," said the doctor gently. "He's very occupied just now you know. You must give him time—" He paused, his words hanging in midair. For the chair in which

Miss M had been sitting was empty, and nothing of her remained in the room save a fragrance of Chanel No 5.

Eighteen months after Argo's launching, Jake signaled that he was running short of food. The scientists were surprised that their calculations on the duration of his provisions should have been so wide of the mark.

"Give reason for extra consumption," they radioed, and Jake replied, "Stowaways."

Dr. Killgruel managed to secure a place on the aircraft which was to parachute fresh supplies; the area chosen was the South Pacific.

Gradually they overhauled Argo; she appeared first as a speck on the shining blue, then as a cobweb or skeleton leaf, and finally as her rakish self, clawing through the water with a bone in her teeth. Slowly the plane gained on her, and at last held steady over her chalk-white decks while the little dandelion puffs fluttered down with their life-saving cargoes of soya, sago, celery, and stout.

Looking through powerful glasses Dr. Killgruel saw Brandywine and his stowaways. Dressed in nothing but a pair of old jeans, with an arm around Miss M, serene in a sarong, Jake sprawled in a hammock, brown as a nut and blissfully happy. Near at hand, like a faithful dinosaur, stood an attendant 93 bus.

# Smell

"Have you put that
it's for a poor old lady who's very hard of hearing and nearly
blind as well? Have you asked them to do it as quick as possible?" said Mrs. Ruffle.

She was a massive old woman; her round, soup-plate hat
encircled a heavy face, fixed in the expression of stony noncom-
munication habitual to the deaf.

"Yes, I told you so twice, I put it," her son said impa-
tiently and then, remembering she could not hear him, gave
several emphatic nods, stooping toward her over the post-office
counter. But she continued to watch him with an intent, peer-

ing, distrustful stare as he folded the letter he had written, tucked it among the wadding in a small sturdy cardboard box, bound up the package with adhesive tape, addressed it in large capitals to HEARING-AID REPAIR DEPARTMENT, Stanbury Ear, Nose, and Throat Hospital, Stanbury, and stuck on a stamp.

"How soon do you think they will send it back, George?"

"Three days, four maybe. *Four* days," he shouted, mouthing the words.

"What do you say, dear?"

He tried to take her hand, to demonstrate by counting on her knobbed, aged fingers, but, physical contact being a rarity with her nowadays, she started back nervously, like a wild animal in hostile surroundings, and by her movement dislodged a tall pyramid of biscuit tins which stood on the floor beside her. Marie, Nice, Oval Osborne, Petit Beurre, Sponge Fingers, all came cascading down onto the uneven brick floor of the little shop. Hardly noticing the chaos she left behind her, Mrs. Ruffle tapped her way, with her heavy white-painted stick, toward the street entrance, through a group of other customers who made solicitous way for her. In the door she paused to sniff disapprovingly and say, "There's something smells not all it should be around here. George! You've let some of the biscuits go mouldy! Not putting the lid on tight, that's what does it. There's mice there, too, if you ask me. I never could fancy a Marie biscuit that's gone soft, that the mice have run over."

George Ruffle, angrily shoveling biscuits, strips of corrugated paper, and shavings off the bricks, made no answer but shrugged in response to sympathetic grins as if to say, "What can you do?" He dumped the spoiled stock in an empty wooden barrel and went back to serving customers behind the counter.

His mother put her head through the door again.

"Your father wouldn't ever have let such a thing happen! Nothing but fresh goods there was in the shop when he was living. None of this frozen stuff then, that costs double the money and doesn't do you a bit of good."

And she directed a short-sighted malignant glance at the deep freeze, installed by George after his father's death in spite of her vehemently expressed objections.

"How often d'you clean that contraption out, anyway? Every other August Bank Holiday? Wouldn't hurt to get that lazy boy of yours to do it once in a blue moon." She gave a grim chuckle and shook off the hand of a man who offered to help her down the two steps into the village street. "Someone around here been fishing by the smell of him," she muttered and tapped her way out of sight.

"Independent old lady, your mother," a farmer said, buying national insurance stamps at the post office counter.

"Independent!" said George. "You can't do a thing with her. The Health Visitor doesn't like her being out there in the cottage on her own, but she won't budge. Says she means to die among her own things, not in an old people's home that's only the workhouse by another name."

"Still, she's good for a tidy few years yet by the look of her."

"Oh, she's as healthy as they come," agreed George, rapping down a pile of coins and sliding them under the grill. "It's just that, being so deaf, she's a bit of a risk on her own— wouldn't hear a pan boil over, or a tap left running. Specially without her aid, like now. Still, what can you do? You can't shift her. She's got enough to live on, she was born in that cottage, and she reckons to die there—Yes, Wally? Postal order for three and eleven? Frank," he called to his son at the back of the shop, "just leave loading up those orders into the van and give a hand at the counter a moment, will you?"

Frank, a handsome, sullen-looking boy in a white overall, dropped the carton of groceries he had just picked up and reluctantly obeyed.

Meanwhile old Mrs. Ruffle slowly pursued her familiar course. Butcher: chopped shin and a bone for the dog. Rendell the chemist: digestive tablets. "No hearing-aid batteries today?" he inquired, but receiving absolutely no response, abandoned the attempt to communicate and handed her the tablets and change, which she carefully counted, feeling the milled edges of the sixpences with her thumbnail.

Two pairs of woollen stockings at Miss Knox's.

"She buys two pairs a month, regular," Miss Knox confided to her visiting cousin when the door closed behind Mrs. Ruffle. "Extravagant, but she says she can't see to mend, and she might as well spend her cash as let it lie."

"She must be nicely off."

"Oh, they say in the village that she's got quite a little nest egg tucked away somewhere in that cottage of hers."

Miss Knox glanced out at the solid old back, slowly retreating along the village street.

Old Mrs. Ruffle tapped her way home by touch, sight within a four-foot radius, and smell. Whiff of scorching hair and cuticle from the blacksmith's. Steep grassy bank in front of the church. Dandelions on it. Church gate, newly painted, with a reek of warm creosote in the June sun. Stretch of yew hedge around the churchyard: a dark, dusty smell. She went through the gate into the old cemetery and checked on Bert's grave;

yes, they had changed the flowers and the grass was clipped; no more than they ought to do, either, but she wouldn't ever be surprised if they left off doing it, George never having shown the proper respect for his father, Doris thinking herself a cut above her husband's family, and Frank a spoiled lazy young scamp, his mind on nothing but lotteries and motorbikes.

After the ritual visit to the grave and ten minutes' rest on the churchyard bench (it bore a plaque In memory of Albert Edward Ruffle, donated by his widow) she went slowly on. Past the Ring of Bells: smell of sawdust and beer through the open door. Down the hill that led from the village on its knoll to the flat salt marshes below. Dark, first, between shady banks. Smell of damp earth and long grass. Then out into the sun again. Tang of ammonia borne along the breeze from the sheep pastured on the marshes beyond the dyke. When she had on her hearing aid, Mrs. Ruffle could just catch their thin, incessant bleating, but now the sound was lost to her, dispersed into the great bright vault of sky. She stumped on, sniffing the salt of the five-mile-distant sea, keeping carefully to the middle of the narrow little flat road between its neatly tended dykes. The only vehicles to pass that way were farm trucks and delivery vans; the drivers were familiar with the sight of her stocky figure ahead of them, and slowed carefully to skirt around her, two wheels on the verge.

Now she began to get the fragrance of her privet hedge, her broad beans in full flower; as she drew nearer home the accustomed smell of the cottage itself came out to greet her: old brickwork, reed thatch, the boiled potatoes of a thousand dinners. Rover the bullterrier lumbered wagging from his kennel —so familiar was his greeting that she almost deceived herself she could hear the joyful rattle of his chain. She gave him the bone, and he settled down to worry it in a patch of dust and sun.

With unerring fingers she reached for the key, hidden on its nail under the thatch—and paused. It was hanging the wrong way around. Muttering distrustfully to herself she took it down, inserted it in the lock, and opened her front door.

The instant she stepped inside she knew that an intruder had been there—might, for all she could hear, be there still. She stood motionless, with dilated eyes and nostrils, desperately straining her blocked ears to listen, until fear and the vain concentration turned her giddy. Only after more than five minutes had gone by did she dare creep tremulously forward, turning her head from side to side like a tortoise, moving across her room from one piece of furniture to the next. Yes! That chair had been shifted, so had the table. The cupboard door was unlatched. She reached in, right to the back, and brought out a small pink lusterware teapot; with shaking fingers removed the lid.

The teapot was empty.

It took Mrs. Ruffle a very long time to assimilate this fact. A dozen, two dozen times she replaced the teapot, took it out again, felt inside it. Then she took out other teapots—jugs, bowls, dishes—and feverishly, uselessly hunted inside each in turn. She ransacked the whole cupboard—the room—the house. She put everything back and then started again. By the third time around she could not be bothered to replace the articles she had moved. There was no strength left in her. She sat down weakly in the bony old armchair that had adapted itself to her shape through forty years of use, and went straight to sleep. In her sleep she twitched and shivered like a dog that dreams of hunting; her hands opened and shut in a ceaseless, obsessive search.

# THE GREEN FLASH

Next morning she woke early and began searching again; then broke off, remembering that Sid the milk boy would soon arrive, and went out to watch for him. As soon as his faded blue pony cart stopped outside she ran out to the gate.

"Sid! I've been robbed! I've been robbed, Sid! You'll have to get the police."

"Are you all right, missis?" Sid was alarmed by her haggard whiteness and vacant, unfixed look; he offered to take her along to George's in the cart, but she ignored the offer, which indeed she had not heard, and finally he drove off, promising to send help right away.

When Constable Trencher came to the cottage she was at first reassured by his imposing dark-blue uniform and bright buttons. He searched the place, from attic bedrooms to the back cellar under the garden that was never used because the septic tank tended to flood into it in wet weather. Everywhere the constable went, Mrs. Ruffle followed.

"How are you going to get the money back?" she kept saying. "How are you going to get back my five hundred pounds? You will get it back, won't you?"

When he tried to explain the obstacles to this outcome: the absence of fingerprints, the lack of clues or witnesses, the fact that, although almost everybody in the village had suspected the existence of her hoard, in fact there was no proof at all that it had amounted to as much as she claimed, or even to a tenth of that figure; when he tried to lecture her on the folly of keeping five hundred pounds in a teapot, she gave no evidence of having heard him, but continued to repeat, "You will get it back, won't you?"

He wondered if she was quite right in the head, if the shock had damaged her wits. At last he appealed for guidance

58

to his superior, Superintendent Bray, who sensibly postponed talking to her until the hospital had sent back her repaired hearing-aid, and communication, if only of a patchy kind, was once more reestablished.

George, angry, embarrassed, touchy, and ashamed, escorted his mother to the police station.

"You realize it was a very foolish act, to keep all that money at home, Mrs. Ruffle?" the superintendent addressed her loudly. "We can't promise to get it back, you know."

"Don't you lecture me, young man!" the old woman snapped. "You just do get it back, that's all I want. He can't spend it yet a while, can he, or the neighbors will get suspicious."

"He?"

"The thief, the one who took it."

"He may have used it to pay a debt outside the district. And we haven't any clue as to who took it at present."

"Well, use your wits, you dumb-headed fool!" "Mother!" said George, scandalized, but Mrs. Ruffle went on undeterred. "It must be someone who comes to the house regular, mustn't it, or Rover would have kicked up a shine. Who comes to the house regular? Well, there's Sid Curtis, with the milk, young Tom Haynes the postman, my grandson Frank brings my groceries once a week, there's my son George here —" "Mother! Really!" "—my daughter-in-law Doris, not that she comes more than once in a month of Sundays, there's Wally Turner reads the electric meter, Bernard Wiggan does a bit of digging for me when the pub's shut, Alf Dunning delivers the coal, and Luke Short and Jim Hamble from the council, they come and empty out my septic tank when it chocks up. So it must be one o' them, mustn't it?"

"That's all very well, missis," the superintendent pointed out, "but that gives us quite a choice, doesn't it? Unless you have any idea which it might be?"

"Oh, I know who it is," she said scornfully. The two men gaped at her.

"What do you mean, you know, Mother? How do you know?"

"I smelled him, didn't I?"

"You *smelled* him?"

"Folks smell different, don't they? You," she said to the superintendent, "you smell of nice clean broadcloth. My son George mostly smells of cheese. Sid Curtis smells of pony. Tom Haynes smells of that flake tobacco he smokes; young Frank reeks of aftershave lotion, you can smell him halfway down the road; same with Wally Turner only with him it's those pigs he keeps; Doris uses white violets scent; Bernard always smells of the chips they fry in the public bar; Alf Dunning smells o' coal and sacking, very strong; Luke and Jim they smell of sewage, poor souls, how their wives can stand it I don't know, but we've all got to live I suppose."

"But how can you possibly be sure?"

"If I'm not sure now," said Mrs. Ruffle, "I'll be sure next time I smell him."

"So which do you think it was?"

"Huh! I'm not telling you," said Mrs. Ruffle cunningly. "Not unless you give me your promise you'll arrest him. Otherwise, what's to stop him cutting my throat first?"

"But, good heavens, we can't arrest somebody just because you say you smelled him," the superintendent exclaimed, irritable with the effort of speaking loud enough to make her hear. "A smell's not evidence."

It took him a morning's arguing to persuade her that he

really did not intend to proceed on her suggestion; when George finally took her home she had lost the temporary vigor induced by her belief that she could convince the superintendent, and relapsed into her state of semishock. She sat listlessly in her armchair, paying no attention to George, who was telling her that now she must certainly leave her cottage and move in with him and Doris. "You can't stay here alone any longer, Mother, do you understand? What'll you live on, for one thing?"

At that she roused up a little and said, "I'll live on my old-age pension, like I always have. I just won't be able to buy any new stockings, that's all. Doris'll have to put up with mending me old ones, whether she likes it or not. Now get along with you George, you haven't been much use, have you? And don't you dare mention what I told that policeman unless you want me murdered in my bed."

She locked up after the disgruntled George and then returned to sit muttering and twitching in her armchair, staring with a set, heavy face into the fire.

A month went by, during which time nobody in the village gave evidence of sudden and suspicious wealth. Various people were questioned by the police, without result; it became plain that the matter was going to be allowed to drop. The regular visitors paid their regular calls at Mrs. Ruffle's cottage: Sid, Frank, Bernard came and went; Alf Dunning delivered coal; Doris made reluctant visits to her mother-in-law with mended stockings; the postman left an occasional card, which Mrs. Ruffle could not read, from her married daughter in Canada. The warm June weather turned to a cold and rainy July; water brimmed along the dykes and lay in pools on the sodden marsh and in Mrs. Ruffle's garden; predictably, her septic tank began to leak an evil-smelling trickle into the cellar, and she sent a message to the council cleansing department asking them to come and pump her out.

And then one day at teatime Wally Turner came to read the electric meter.

It had been a dark, sodden afternoon; rain endlessly trickled off the thatch and overflowed from Mrs. Ruffle's rainwater barrel; the saturated sheep huddled together and cried dolefully out on the marsh; Rover dozed in his kennel and Mrs. Ruffle sat by a fistful of fire brooding about her empty teapot. Even now, she still sometimes momentarily believed that she might have been mistaken about her loss, and she would take the teapot from the cupboard, lift the lid, and peer wistfully inside, as if a bundle of notes might suddenly materialize there.

When Wally's knock came, Mrs. Ruffle was in the back kitchen, putting on the kettle. Accustomed to open the door and walk in if she did not answer, Wally did so on this occasion and made his way through to the narrow passage where the meter was awkwardly sited in a dark corner under the stairs, beside the cellar door.

"Good afternoon, Wally." Mrs. Ruffle's voice behind his shoulder made him start; she was wearing felt slippers, and he had not heard her come out of the kitchen.

"Hello, there, Mrs. Ruffle," he said loudly and nervously. "Not got through quite so much current then, this time, by the look."

"That's just as well, isn't it? Now all my savings are stolen, I need to cut down on spending."

"I was sorry to hear about that, Mrs. Ruffle," he shouted.

"Were you, Wally?" She came up close to him and with apparent irrelevance asked, "How are the pigs, then?" Her nostrils twitched slightly.

# Smell

"Not so bad, Mrs. Ruffle, but they don't like this weather."

"Who does? I'm worried about my cellar, I can tell you; if the council don't come soon it's going to fill right up. Have a look at it, Wally, and say if you think the water's going to fuse my electric."

"Oh, it ought to be all right," he said, "your wiring doesn't go through the cellar, does it?"

"Just the same, I wish you'd look and see, Wally."

She unlocked the cellar door and opened it, letting out a dismaying stench of wet decay. With reluctance, Wally peered down the dark steps.

"Can you see where the water's got to?"

"It's too dark," he said.

"Your eyes'll get used to it in a moment. Take a step down inside."

He took a step down, she put the end of her stick against his back and gave a powerful shove. Slipping on the wet stone, he fell forward into the dark with a desperate cry, and a splash.

Mrs. Ruffle shut and relocked the door.

"That'll teach you to help yourself to other folk's savings," she shouted through the keyhole, and went back into the kitchen to finish making tea.

Wally, who had broken his leg, managed to drag himself painfully out of two feet of foul-smelling water and up the cellar stairs.

"It wasn't me, it wasn't me!" he moaned, beating on the door with his fists. And then, much later, "Anyway, you can't prove it, you bloody old hag! You'll never see your money again."

Mrs. Ruffle paid no attention. His shouts were audible

63

only at the back of the cottage, and not very distinctly even there; in any case, she had switched off her hearing aid, and, after some consideration, dropped it from a height on the brick floor.

Next afternoon she plodded up to the post office, through the rain.

"You'll have to send this thing back to the hospital, George," she said. "It's gone wrong again." She watched impassively while he parceled and dispatched it.

Luke Short was in the shop, and she said, "When's the council going to come and pump out my septic, Luke? The cellar's half full of water as it is; another few days of this weather, and it'll be up to the top of the steps."

"Very sorry, Mrs. Ruffle," Luke bawled at the top of his powerful lungs. "We've had such a lot of calls, I reckon we're not liable to get around to you for another four or five days at least; say next Thursday."

Uncertain whether she had understood, he took down the big post office calendar, held it under her nose, and pointed to Thursday's date. Following his finger, she nodded slowly. ·

"Thursday? I'll have to be satisfied with that, then, shan't I? Thursday ought to just about do."

And she hobbled slowly off down the village.

It rained for another week. After three days Mrs. Ruffle decided that she could unlock the cellar door. By now the stench was noticeable even when the door was shut.

So she did not bother to open it and look inside.

# Searching for Summer

Lily wore yellow on her wedding day. In the 'eighties people put a lot of faith in omens, and believed that if a bride's dress was yellow her married life would be blessed with a bit of sunshine.

It was years since the bombs had been banned but still the cloud never lifted. Whitish gray, day after day, sometimes darkening to a weeping slate-color, or, at the end of an evening, turning to smoky copper, the sky endlessly, secretively brooded.

Old people began their stories with the classic, fairy-tale opening: "Long, long ago, when I was a liddle un, in the days when the sky was blue . . ." and children, listening, chuckled among themselves at the absurd thought, because, *blue*, imagine it! How could the sky ever have been *blue?* You might as well say, "In the days when the grass was pink."

Stars, rainbows, and all other such heavenly sideshows had been permanently withdrawn, and if the radio announced that there was a blink of sunshine in such and such a place, where the cloud belt had thinned for half an hour, cars and buses would pour in that direction for days in an unavailing search for warmth and light.

After the wedding, when all the relations were standing on the church porch, with Lily shivering prettily in her buttercup nylon, her father prodded the dour and withered grass on a grave—although it was August the leaves were hardly out yet —and said, "Well, Tom, what are you aiming to do now, eh?"

"Going to find a bit of sun and have our honeymoon in it," said Tom. There was a general laugh from the wedding party.

"Don't get sunburned," shrilled Aunt Nancy.

"Better start off Bournemouth way. Paper said they had a half hour of sun last Wednesday week," Uncle Arthur weighed in heavily.

"We'll come back brown as—as this grass," said Tom, and ignoring the good-natured teasing from their respective families, the two young people mounted on their scooter, which stood ready at the churchyard wall, and chugged away in a shower of golden confetti. When they were out of sight, and the yellow paper had subsided on the gray and gritty road, the Whitemores and the Hoskinses strolled off, sighing, to eat wedding cake and drink currant wine, and old Mrs. Hoskins spoiled everyone's pleasure by bursting into tears as she thought of her own wedding day when everything was so different.

Meanwhile Tom and Lily buzzed on hopefully across the gray countryside, with Lily's veil like a gilt banner floating behind. It was chilly going for her in her wedding things, but the sight of a bride was supposed to bring good luck and so she stuck it out, although her fingers were blue to the knuckles. Every now and then they switched on their portable radio and listened to the forecast. Inverness had seen the sun for ten minutes yesterday, and Southend for five minutes this morning, but that was all.

"Both those places are a long way from here," said Tom cheerfully. "All the more reason we'd find a nice bit of sunshine in these parts somewhere. We'll keep on going south. Keep your eyes peeled, Lil, and tell me if you see a blink of sun on those hills ahead."

But they came to the hills and passed them, and a new range shouldered up ahead and then slid away behind, and still there was no flicker or patch of sunshine to be seen anywhere in the gray, winter-ridden landscape. Lilly began to get discouraged, so they stopped for a cup of tea at a drive-in.

"Seen the sun lately, mate?" Tom asked the proprietor.

He laughed shortly. "Notice any buses or trucks around here? Last time I saw the sun was two years ago September; came out just in time for the wife's birthday."

"It's stars I'd like to see," Lily said, looking wistfully at her dust-colored tea. "Ever so pretty they must be."

"Well, better be getting on I suppose," said Tom, but he had lost some of his bounce and confidence. Every place they passed through looked nastier than the last, partly on account of the dismal light, partly because people had given up bothering to take a pride in their boroughs. And then, just as they were entering a village called Molesworth, the dimmest, drabbest, most insignificant huddle of houses they had come to yet, the engine coughed and died on them.

"Can't see what's wrong," said Tom, after a prolonged and gloomy survey.

"Oh, Tom!" Lily was almost crying. "What'll we do?"

"Have to stop here for the night, s'pose." Tom was short-tempered with frustration. "Look, there's a garage just up the road. We can push the bike there, and they'll tell us if there's a pub where we can stay. It's nearly six anyway."

They had taken the bike to the garage, and the man there was just telling them that the only pub in the village was the Rising Sun, where Mr. Noakes might be able to give them a bed, when a bus pulled up in front of the petrol pumps.

"Look," the garage owner said, "there's Mr. Noakes just getting out of the bus now. Sid!" he called.

But Mr. Noakes was not able to come to them at once. Two old people were climbing slowly out of the bus ahead of him: a blind man with a white stick, and a withered, frail old lady in a black satin dress and hat. "Careful now, George," she was saying, "mind ee be careful with my son William."

"I'm being careful, Mrs. Hatching," the conductor said patiently, as he almost lifted the unsteady old pair off the bus platform. The driver had stopped his engine, and everyone on the bus was taking a mild and sympathetic interest, except for Mr. Noakes just behind who was cursing irritably at the delay. When the two old people were on the narrow pavement, the conductor saw that they were going to have trouble with a bicycle that was propped against the curb just ahead of them; he picked it up and stood holding it until they had passed the line of petrol pumps and were going slowly off along a path across the fields. Then, grinning, he put it back, jumped hurriedly into the bus, and rang his bell.

"Old nuisances," Mr. Noakes said furiously. "Wasting public time. Every week that palaver goes on, taking the old man to Midwick Hospital Out Patients and back again. I know what I'd do with 'em. Put to sleep, that sort ought to be."

Mr. Noakes was a repulsive-looking individual, but when he heard that Tom and Lily wanted a room for the night, he changed completely and gave them a leer that was full of false goodwill. He was a big, red-faced man with wet, full lips, bulging pale-gray bloodshot eyes, and a crop of stiff greasy black hair. He wore tennis shoes.

"Honeymooners, eh?" he said, looking sentimentally at Lily's pale prettiness. "Want a bed for the night, eh?" and he laughed a disgusting laugh that sounded like thick oil coming out of a bottle, heh-heh-heh-heh, and gave Lily a tremendous pinch on her arm. Disengaging herself as politely as she could, she stooped and picked up something from the pavement. They followed Mr. Noakes glumly up the street to the Rising Sun.

While they were eating their baked beans, Mr. Noakes stood over their table grimacing at them. Lily unwisely confided to him that they were looking for a bit of sunshine. Mr. Noakes's laughter nearly shook down the ramshackle building.

"Sunshine! Oh my gawd! That's a good 'un! Hear that, Mother?" he bawled to his wife. "They're looking for a bit of sunshine. Heh-heh-heh-heh-heh-heh! Why," he said, banging on the table till the baked beans leaped about, "if I could find a bit of sunshine near here, permanent bit that is, dja know what I'd do?"

The young people looked at him inquiringly across the bread and margarine.

"Lido, trailer-site, country club, holiday camp—you wouldn't know the place. Land around here is dirt cheap, I'd buy up the lot. Nothing but woods. I'd advertise—I'd have people flocking to this little dump from all over the country.

But what a hope, what a hope, eh? Well, feeling better? Enjoyed your tea? Ready for bed? Heh-heh-heh-heh, bed's ready for you."

Avoiding one another's eyes, Tom and Lily stood up.

"I—I'd like to go for a bit of a walk first, Tom," Lily said in a small voice. "Look, I picked up that old lady's bag on the pavement, I didn't notice it till we'd done talking to Mr. Noakes, and by then she was out of sight. Should we take it back to her?"

"Good idea," said Tom, pouncing on the suggestion with relief. "Do you know where she lives, Mr. Noakes?"

"Who, old Ma Hatching? Sure I know. She lives in the wood. But you don't want to go taking her bag back, not this time o' the evening you don't. Let her worry. She'll come asking for it in the morning."

"She walked so slowly," said Lily, holding the bag gently in her hands. It was very old, made of black velvet on two ring-handles, and embroidered with beaded roses. "I think we ought to take it to her, don't you, Tom?"

"Oh, very well, very well, have it your own way," Mr. Noakes said, winking at Tom. "Take that path by the garage, you can't go wrong. I've never been there meself, but they live somewhere in that wood back o' the village, you'll find it soon enough."

They found the path soon enough, but not the cottage. Under the lowering sky they walked forward endlessly among trees that carried only tiny and rudimentary leaves, wizened and poverty stricken. Lily was still wearing her wedding sandals, which had begun to blister her. She held onto Tom's arm, biting her lip with the pain, and he looked down miserably at her bent brown head; everything had turned out so differently from what he had planned.

70

By the time they reached the cottage Lily could hardly bear to put her left foot to the ground, and Tom was gentling her along: "It can't be much farther now, and they'll be sure to have a bandage. I'll tie it up, and you can have a sit-down. Maybe they'll give us a cup of tea. We could borrow an old pair of socks or something. . . ." Hardly noticing the cottage garden, beyond a vague impression of rows of runner beans, they made for the clematis-grown porch and knocked. There was a brass lion's head on the door, carefully polished.

"Eh, me dear!" It was the old lady, old Mrs. Hatching, who opened the door, and her exclamation was a long-drawn gasp of pleasure and astonishment. "Eh, me dear! 'Tis the pretty bride. See'd ye s'arternoon when we was coming home from hospital."

"Who be?" shouted a voice from inside.

"Come in, come in, me dears. My son William'll be glad to hear company; he can't see, poor soul, nor has this thirty year, ah, and a pretty sight he's losing this minute—"

"We brought back your bag," Tom said, putting it in her hands, "and we wondered if you'd have a bit of plaster you could kindly let us have. My wife's hurt her foot—"

My wife. Even in the midst of Mrs. Hatching's voluble welcome the strangeness of these words struck the two young people, and they fell quiet, each of them, pondering, while Mrs. Hatching thanked and commiserated, all in a breath, and asked them to take a seat on the sofa and fetched a basin of water from the scullery, and William from his seat in the chimney corner demanded to know what it was all about.

"Wot be doing? Wot be doing, Mother?"

" 'Tis a bride, all in's finery," she shrilled back at him, "an's blistered her foot, poor heart." Keeping up a running commentary for William's benefit she bound up the foot, every

71

now and then exclaiming to herself in wonder over the fineness
of Lily's wedding dress, which lay in yellow nylon swathes
around the chair. "There, me dear. Now us'll have a cup of tea,
eh? Proper thirsty you'm fare to be, walking all the way to here
this hot day."

Hot day? Tom and Lily stared at each other and then
around the room. Then it was true, it was not their imagination, that a great dusty golden square of sunshine lay on the
fireplace wall, where the brass pendulum of the clock at every
swing blinked into sudden brilliance? That the blazing geraniums on the windowsill housed a drove of murmuring bees?
That, through the window the gleam of linen hung in the sun
to whiten suddenly dazzled their eyes?

"The sun? Is it really the sun?" Tom said, almost doubtfully.

"And why not?" Mrs. Hatching demanded. "How else'll
beans set, tell me that? Fine thing if sun were to stop shining.
Chuckling to herself she set out a Crown Derby tea set, gor-
geously colored in red and gold, and a baking of saffron buns.
Then she sat down and, drinking her own tea, began to question the two of them about where they had come from, where
they were going. The tea was tawny and hot and sweet; the
clock's tick was like a bird chirping; every now and then a log
settled in the grate; Lily looked sleepily around the little room,
so rich and peaceful, and thought, I wish we were staying here,
I wish we needn't go back to that horrible pub. . . . She leaned
against Tom's comforting arm.

"Look at the sky," she whispered to him. "Out there between the geraniums. Blue!"

"And ee'll come up and see my spare bedroom, won't ee
now?" Mrs. Hatching said, breaking off the thread of her ques-

tions—which indeed was not a thread, but merely a savoring of her pleasure and astonishment at this unlooked-for visit—"Bide here, why don't ee? Mid as well. The lil un's fair wore out. Us'll do for ee better 'n rangy old Noakes, proper old scoundrel 'e be. Won't us, William?"

"Ah," William said appreciatively. "I'll sing ee some o' my songs."

A sight of the spare room settled any doubts. The great white bed, huge as a prairie, built up with layer upon solid layer of mattress, blanket, and quilt, almost filled the little shadowy room in which it stood. Brass rails shone in the green dimness. "Isn't it quiet," Lily whispered. Mrs. Hatching, silent for the moment, stood looking at them proudly, her bright eyes slowly moving from face to face. Once her hand fondled, as if it might have been a baby's downy head, the yellow brass knob.

And so, almost without any words, the matter was decided.

Three days later they remembered that they must go to the village and collect the scooter which must, surely, be mended by now.

They had been helping old William pick a basketful of beans. Tom had taken his shirt off, and the sun gleamed on his brown back; Lily was wearing an old cotton print which Mrs. Hatching, with much chuckling, had shortened to fit her.

It was amazing how deftly, in spite of his blindness, William moved among the beans, feeling through the rough, rustling leaves for the stiffness of concealed pods. He found twice as many as Tom and Lily, but then they, even on the third day, were still stopping every other minute to exclaim over the blueness of the sky. At night they sat on the back doorstep while

Mrs. Hatching clucked inside as she dished the supper, "Star struck ee'll be! Come along in, do-ee, before soup's cold, star niver run away yet as I do know."

"Can we get anything for you in the village?" Lily asked, but Mrs. Hatching shook her head.

"Baker's bread and suchlike's no use but to cripple thee's innardses wi' colic. I been living here these eighty year wi'out troubling doctors, and I'm not faring to begin now." She waved to them and stood watching as they walked into the wood, thin and frail beyond belief, but wiry, indomitable, her black eyes full of zest. Then she turned to scream menacingly at a couple of pullets who had strayed and were scratching among the potatoes.

Almost at once they noticed, as they followed the path, that the sky was clouded over.

"It *is* only there on that one spot," Lily said in wonder. "All the time. And they've never even noticed that the sun doesn't shine in other places."

"That's how it must have been all over the world once," Tom said.

At the garage they found their scooter ready and wait ing. They were about to start back when they ran into Mr. Noakes.

"Well, well, well, well, *well!*" he shouted, glaring at them with ferocious good humor. "How many wells make a river, eh? And where did you slip off to? Here's me and the missus was just going to tell the police to have the rivers dragged. But hullo, hullo, what's this? Brown, eh? Suntan? Scrumptious," he said, looking meltingly at Lily and giving her another tremen dous pinch. "Where'd you get it, eh? That wasn't all got in half an hour, *I* know. Come on, this means money to you and me,

74

tell us the big secret. Remember what I said, land around these parts is dirt cheap."

Tom and Lily looked at each other in horror. They thought of the cottage, the bees humming among the runner-beans, the sunlight glinting in the red-and-gold teacups. At night, when they had lain in the huge sagging bed, stars had shone through the window and the whole wood was as quiet as the inside of a shell.

"Oh, we've been miles from here," Tom lied hurriedly. "We ran into a friend, and he took us right away beyond Brinsley." And as Mr. Noakes still looked suspicious and un-satisfied, he did the only thing possible. "We're going back there now," he said, "the sunbathing's grand." And opening the throttle he let the scooter go. They waved at Mr. Noakes and chugged off toward the gray hills that lay to the north.

"My wedding dress," Lily said sadly. "It's on our bed."

They wondered how long Mrs. Hatching would keep tea hot for them, who would eat all the pasties.

"Never mind, you won't need it again," Tom comforted her.

At least, he thought, they had left the golden place un-disturbed. Mr. Noakes never went into the wood. And they had done what they intended, they had found the sun. Now they, too, would be able to tell their grandchildren, when be-ginning a story, "Long, long ago, when we were young, in the days when the sky was blue. . . ."

# A View of the Heath

It was one of those summer Saturdays when the scent of may drifting along the quiet London streets was so warm and spicy that you could almost lean against it. Not a soul was to be seen in Willow Crescent as I walked home, apart from a stately tabby—if a cat is a soul—dozing on a stone gatepost. Everybody was out on the Heath. The laburnums and lilacs blazed unregarded, and all the front gardens were rich and silent and alive—even the immense carved stone acorns, bigger than footballs, with which some nineteenth-century architect had decorated each pair of front steps in the crescent looked as if they might soon burgeon into megatherium-sized cotyledons.

## A View of the Heath

I was feeling pretty good. I was in my twenties, and the century was in its twenties, and I'd just bought a house, and my business was doing well. But principally here it was, the best Saturday of the summer, with the bookshop closed till Monday, and nothing to do but mow the lawn and watch the baby kick on a rug. Over the page Sunday stretched clean and empty and sparkling, ready for us to follow our fancy, go for a drive, or picnic on the Heath, or just stay at home in our own garden and nibble at our own slice of the season studded with daffodils like decorations on a cake.

When I rounded the curve at the head of the Crescent I saw, far away below me, nearly at the foot, an old lady coming toward me. She seemed to be the only other person in Hampstead, and to have come out of my own front gate, though at that distance it was hard to be certain. She came quickly up the hill, almost running, and smiling to herself as if she had seen something pleasant. She was dressed in gray and had a hat with a bunch of cherries on it, nonsensical, but under it her face, now it was close enough to study, was one of the most remarkable I'd ever come across, though all I really noticed in the moment when we passed was wide cheekbones like a ballerina's, that sweet inscrutable smile, and brilliant eyes. Her gray hair was short, shingled, and she had very neat little feet.

As we passed she nodded at me and said, "Isn't it a lovely day!" and I said yes to that. I went on down to my house and let myself in with my latchkey. It was so new that the action was still a self-conscious one. The front hall was cool and dark and smelled of prunus leaves. I thought Rose would be in the garden, but she came out of the sitting room and put her arms around my neck, and said, "You're going to be cross with me."

"Why?"

# THE GREEN FLASH

"I've let the attic. To a woman."

I had laid down an ultimatum that no tenant was to be fixed on unless I was there to do the fixing, and that, whatever other characteristics he might have, he was to be a man. Women lodgers, I said, always ended up as part of the family, and probably a regrettable part; male lodgers led their own independent lives and that was that.

"She's just gone," Rose said. "You've just missed her. Her name is Miss Ross."

I thought of all the things it was essential to say about the structure and fabric of our marriage, and how it was important to adhere to any mutually agreed arrangements or there'd be no basis for trust and affection. I had it sorted, ready to bring out in one splendid sentence peppered with semicolons, and then I noticed how Rose was smiling at me. Sweet and inscrutable. The sentence exploded in my mind like a puffball, and I kissed her instead—she smelled warm and spicy like the mayblossom—and she rubbed her cheek against mine and said, "Take your jacket off, it's hot. I've put out your dark blue shirt. Oh, isn't it lovely having so much *time.*"

"Was Miss Ross the one with the cherries on her hat?" I asked, going upstairs.

"Yes, that one. Her stuff's coming on Monday."

It was sunny all weekend and fine still on Monday. I took the morning off from the bookshop in case my help was needed with moving the things, but I needn't have bothered. They consisted of three suitcases, a bundle of umbrellas and walking sticks, tied up very neatly, two wooden chests like schoolboys' trunks, and a couple of packages in waterproof sheeting. We took them upstairs and put them in the attic ready for Miss Ross.

Rose had had fun doing up the attic. She had distem-

78

ered the walls white, with a faint trace of pink, and had found
ome pink-and-white striped chintz for curtains and cushions.
She'd painted the wicker armchair a dark glossy blue.

"Miss Ross loved it," she said. "She looked all about
and said, 'I'm so glad there's a view of the Heath. I couldn't
have taken it otherwise,' and counted the drawers, and stroked
he curtains a little with her finger, and then she smiled at me,
hat two-edged smile of hers, you know—"

"I know."

"—and said, 'You've made this a happy room, my dear.'
Then we went downstairs and Nancy brought her a cup of tea
because it was such a hot afternoon, and she picked up
Amanda and asked when her birthday was, and then she said
he'd like to take the room and would send her things around
on Monday."

"She didn't say when she'd arrive herself?"

Rose shook her head. "I gave her a key. I expect she'll
come tomorrow."

But we didn't see Miss Ross again for twenty years.

She paid her rent on the dot. Regularly, without fail, by
he first post on the first of each month a check for eight
pounds would arrive from an address in Kensington, and I'd
send the receipt back there. And from time to time boxes and
parcels addressed to Miss Ross were delivered, and we put
hem up in her room, which became a little more cluttered as
he years went by, but remained basically unchanged. We never
used the room. Occasionally we'd borrow the armchair or the
able lamp from it, but they always went back again. It was
called Miss Ross's room, and it was very definitely alien terri-
ory, though not unfriendly. Indeed when Amanda got to be
six or seven, she used to go and sit there quietly sometimes, by
herself; she said it gave her a mysterious feeling.

# THE GREEN FLASH

I think we all borrowed it as a hiding place occasionally when we wanted to sort ourselves out from the kaleidoscope of family life. Naturally we used to wonder a good deal what was in the boxes, and one of our favorite fireside games, a variant of "I went to market," was called Miss Ross's boxes.

"I opened Miss Ross's boxes and I found—"

"—a hippopotamus."

"I opened Miss Ross's boxes, and I found a hippopotamus and four bottles of champagne."

"I opened Miss Ross's boxes, and I found a hippopotamus and four bottles of champagne, and a bunch of red roses and a copy of the Koran bound in marble."

"I opened Miss Ross's boxes and I found—"

Of course we never did open them.

It's a queer thing to own a house with one small, separate empty room in it that doesn't belong to you; quite different from having an outsider actually living under your roof. In a way it's salutary, a reminder; it makes you remember how much of your own being is, as it were, unexplored territory.

Every year at Christmas Miss Ross sent us a card, and she sent a present to Nancy who had brought her the tea—generally soap. When Nancy left to get married I wrote and told Miss Ross, and she gave Nancy a wedding present—a salad bowl, I think. Her presents to Amanda were the glorification of birthdays each year; at first it was woolly toys, and a Spanish doll, and a horse on wheels; then later a musical box, a morocco writing case, a little crystal clock . . .

"It's like having a fairy godmother," Amanda said, and the others might have envied her, only Rose took care that they all had special treats on their birthdays. The four younger ones had come along by then: Robin, Tony, Emma, and Bridget.

When Bridget was born, we decided we'd have to move to a bigger house, though we hated leaving Willow Crescent. But I was lucky enough to find a house in Highgate, Grove End Lane, still with a view of the Heath.

At about this time our monthly checks from Miss Ross had started coming from an address in Cornwall, so I wrote to her there and asked if she wanted to keep a room in the new house. She wrote back and asked if it had a view of the Heath, and when I told her yes, she said she'd like to keep it. So I sent her the new latchkey, done up in a little box like wedding cake, and she returned her old one, nice and shiny. We settled down again, and the years went on free-wheeling by. Miss Ross's spiky handwriting on the first of each month was a tiny, essential part of our lives, like the triangle score in a piece of rather comprehensive orchestration.

And then one day we had a letter from her on the fifteenth of the month.

It was addressed to Rose, and I saw her slip back a little, out of the chatter and tinkle of schoolday breakfast, and read it to herself. I was all agog with curiosity to know what was in it, and so were Amanda and the youngsters.

"Do tell, Mummy? Is she coming to visit us?"

"Mandy wants a chance to say thank you for all those presents and make a fresh impression—"

"Miss Ross will probably take one look at her—"

"And say, 'Those aren't the baby legs I saw kicking on a rug.' "

"But tell me, who is this handsome lad?"

"Oh, shut up you oafs," Amanda said cheerfully. "What is it, Mummy?"

## THE GREEN FLASH

"Poor Miss Ross. She's very ill, in an Old People's Home in Canterbury. She wants me to go and see her."

Rose looked at her watch, always a preface to instant action. I said I'd drive her down, and call in on the branch bookshop I'd opened there. The children dispersed to school and Amanda to the Royal Academy of Dramatic Arts.

Rose never told me very much about that visit. She came away from it with a curiously peaceful, recollected expression, like a person who has seen a sunset in the desert, or some such natural marvel. She said Miss Ross hadn't changed in the least degree; during the long, quiet progress from fifty to seventy it is often remarkable how little physical change takes place.

"Her eyes and smile were just the same; only she looked a little tired, because she's having trouble with her heart, it seems."

"What did she want to see you for, Rosie?"

But that Rose could not, or would not, say. Miss Ross had not spoken about herself a great deal, I gathered; she had asked many questions about all of us, the children, Amanda, the new house, my business, the book trade—every mortal thing—and made pertinent comments.

"And then when it was time to go," Rose said, "she kissed me and asked if there was anything that I wanted and hadn't got. I said another forty years as good as the last forty, and she burst out laughing and said she couldn't help me there. Then they brought her tea, so I had to go."

"Did she look well cared for, happy?"

"Very happy," said Rose.

Two weeks later I had a typewritten note from the Pinewoods Residential Home—what kind of home isn't residential,

I wonder?—to say that Miss Ross had passed peacefully away and she had left a letter for me.

The handwriting was very shaky indeed, and it took Rose and me a long time to decipher it. She told us to do what we liked with all the things in her room, except for the black suit, which she asked us to give to Mr. Lion Warren.

"The playwright," said Rose in surprise. "Fancy her knowing *him*."

Amanda was thrilled. She was going through a Lion Warren phase, had seen all his plays and practically knew them by heart. Added to this, he lived in Highgate not far away, and she at once began to weave romantic fantasies on the theme of his coming to the house and being struck dumb at her beauty.

"Shouldn't think *he'd* say thank you for a mouldy secondhand black suit," said Tony.

That afternoon we went up to sort Miss Ross's possessions and find the black suit. It was a saddish business. It seemed somehow sacrilegious to be callously winnowing through her things, deciding what was worth keeping and what was junk. There was a fantastic quantity of junk. Box after box contained empty medicine bottles, scrupulously washed; clean, folded paper bags and empty cardboard containers; dozens of little cashbooks holding her daily accounts for twenty years, itemized down to the last farthing.

"It's horrible," said Rose, tears in her eyes. "No one should be allowed to see into another person's life like this."

"I'm sure Miss Ross would be the last person to mind," I pointed out.

We had been wondering if we should consult a lawyer and try to discover whether Miss Ross had left a proper will, but in the circumstances it hardly seemed worth it.

"There's nothing of any value here," I said.

"We haven't found the black suit yet."

I opened one of the cases and saw that it held clothes, but women's clothes, and all dating from the twenties: cloche hats, straight, brilliantly colored dresses, embroidered all over, with scalloped hemlines; rolls and rolls of colored silk stockings, blue, green, black, white, all good as new. Bridget and Emma begged to be allowed to try them on, but Amanda pounced on them and wouldn't let them be played with. Next month we sold most of them for about six hundred pounds; they were used in the production of Under Your Cloche.

We still hadn't found a black suit, though.

"Dolts that we are," Rose said suddenly. "She didn't mean black suit, she meant black suitcase. That was what the squiggle after the 't' was."

The black suitcase was the only one we hadn't tried, so I opened it. My heart sank when I saw rolls and bundles of paper.

"Oh heavens. It's probably receipts for all the bills she ever paid," Rose said. But it wasn't. It was five-pound notes, securities, share certificates, bearer-bonds, Manchester City Bonds—I dug through the case with hands suddenly gone cold and trembling, and estimated that there must be roughly twenty thousand pounds' worth. It had been sitting in our house all these years! Supposing there had been a fire. Or the rain had come through the roof and rotted the paper. Or mice had nibbled through the case. Or it had been lost in the move.

"For heaven's sake," said Rose, "ring up Warren at once. I shan't sleep easy until that case is out of the house. We'll finish sorting the other things and then go and have baths to get rid of the dust."

## A View of the Heath

I went downstairs and looked up his number in the telephone book. When he answered I told him that I was holding a case for him which had belonged to the late Miss Helen Ross, and that I would be grateful if he could have it collected as soon as possible, since the contents were, I believed, rather valuable.

"Can't you have it sent?" he asked irritably.

"I'd very much prefer to hand it to you personally. Of course I can bring it around if it's not convenient for you to come—"

"No, no, I'll come, I'll come," he cut me off, and in ten minutes his large gray car stopped in front of the house. I had seen it before; he sometimes came to the bookshop and bought a casual twenty pounds' worth of books. He ran up the steps as if he would be glad to get the business over quickly; his thin, patrician face wore a permanent look of preoccupied condemnation, as if he were so far withdrawn from life that the circumstances he was actually considering with such censure were some twenty years in the past.

I took him up to the attic, explaining as succinctly as I could how we had come to be connected with Miss Ross. He nodded, glancing with dislike at the pink cheeks and fair heads of Robin and Emma, who lay on their stomachs on the nursery landing reading fairy tales. Amanda met us on the last flight of stairs; she was flushed and dusty, and clasped the large pile of Warren's own plays, new and uncut, that we had found among Miss Ross's things: *Arctic Circle*, *Tangent Out of Nowhere*, *Parallel to Pegasus* could all plainly be seen. She looked delightful, even under the dust; as an entrance it could not, one imagined, have been bettered, but Warren perceptibly flinched, and when I murmured, "This is my eldest daughter,

Amanda," he gave again that brief, ungracious inclination of the head and almost brushed past her.

Amanda darted a glance of disappointment and ran on down the stairs; she dropped the books on the landing and could be heard calling the twins to come and help her bathe Barnabas.

Rose was still in the attic, lovely as an absent-minded Ceres with fluff in her hair. She was smiling to herself over something Amanda had said.

"I managed to get most of the dust off the case for you, Mr. Warren," she told him when he had acknowledged her introduction with thinly veiled impatience. Then giving him a compassionate look she left the room.

"It's very kind of you," Warren repeated. He picked up the case and obviously intended leaving with it at once, but I stopped him.

"I'd feel easier, Mr. Warren, if you'd just glance at the contents of the case and then look at the things in this room. Miss Ross said we could have everything else, but I wouldn't like," I hesitated "—please take anything if it reminds you of her."

With an expression of the utmost distaste, he glanced inside the case; then he became pale and his lips thinned.

"Good heavens," he said. "You have seen these, Mr.—er?"

"Yes," I said.

In some embarrassment he shuffled among the documents, and then looked around the room.

"Is there anything you'd like?" I said.

"No. No I'm sure there's not. This is very good of you, Mr. . . . er," he said. "Well . . ." He picked up the case and moved toward the door. I didn't try to detain him any longer, but he waited another moment, looking questioningly at the glossy blue armchair, the candy-striped curtains, the view between them of the Heath, dusty and golden as the coast of Arabia. There we both stood, two middle-aged men, motionless, at a loss, perhaps a little pathetic, while somewhere the ghost of Miss Ross smiled over that extra piece of knowledge acquired by Eve before Adam came running to the orchard, which she had held over his head ever since.

Bridget and Tony came in as if they had been catapulted. They were to have Miss Ross's attic for a playroom. We left them to it.

In the front hall Robin, Emma, and Amanda were lovingly clustered round the dripping Barnabas, drying him with a towel apiece while he bore it in mournful spaniel fortitude.

"Tea won't be long," Rose called from the kitchen.

"You have a large family," Lion Warren said with a frosty smile, managing to convey that to him all this swarming activity had about as much appeal as a growth of fungus. "Well, let me say again how greatly I am obliged to you. I feel I should do something—is there anything—"

"Oh," I said, my eye on Amanda's pink, averted cheek, "thank you; that's very kind of you; I'd love a couple of seats for your next play."

He said of course he would send tickets, ran out, jumped into his car, and drove quickly away.

"Well!" said Rose, coming out, rubbing floury hands. "My dear, what a dreary, bloodless man. I've never known anyone take such an instant dislike to me."

"But why should Miss Ross have left him all that money?"

"Oh, she told me that when she was young she was engaged to someone, but he broke it off because she was so rich and he wanted to make his own way. I suppose it was him."

"I see. Poor Miss Ross."

"Oh I don't know," said Rose, going back into her kitchen, from which the scent of gingerbread was beginning to breathe out like a blessing. "Think of being married to that bit of desiccated string."

When, two months later, Warren sent me front-row seats for the first night of *Bitter Rectangle*, it was quite a problem to know what to do with them. Amanda had got over her Warren phase, Rose, who loathes his plays, said she'd rather pass the evening doing her mending, so that is why I coaxed out my old aunt Teresa and am sitting here with her waiting for the curtain to go up. I shall be glad to get home.

# Belle of the Ball

Easter came late that
year. The first summer horse race was on Easter Monday, and I
came over from Brighton for it, idling along in the train. Trains
didn't go fast in those days, and you could hear cuckoos see-
sawing in and out of the woods as we made our leisurely way,
and twice as loud when we stopped.

It was one of those bright blowy days with bits of toffee
paper everywhere, kids with their candy ribbons whipped out
of their hands, feathers blowing and swooping on the big,
oyster-shaped hats that all the women were wearing that year.
Down on the front it must have been a regular gale but, of

course, up at the racetrack it was a bit more sheltered by the downs.

You hardly noticed the downs at first, with all the running and shouting and carrying-on, and the laughing and whistles and rattles, old fellows wagging their sausage-balloons, girls trying to hold down their skirts and squealing when the paper streamers tangled around their legs—and then you'd look up and see a greenish-gray shoulder of hill sloping away, as if someone had his back turned on the whole affair.

It's a pretty part. I love it. Still do.

I was over for the day, thinking I'd pick up a bit of money, which was always short with me at that time. I was young, and my blood was quick-circulating and kept me restless; nothing seemed to last with me very long, and cash no time at all.

I suppose on an everyday Monday the High Street would be quiet as a riverbed, but that afternoon it was like bedlam with traffic—some cars, but mostly carts and carriages —jammed from the bridge right up to the castle. They used to keep a thundering great white cockatoo at the hotel in those days, tame, and it was out and flying up and down the street like a zeppelin, rowing on those great brawny wings; every time it passed over there'd be an oo! from the crowd, and women would duck and scream. It flew so low you could see the mad orange glare of its eye; I daresay it thought we were all a bit cuckoo, too.

It was a big help to me, that bird. I'd fixed on the handkerchief game and I was working my way slowly up from the station to the racetrack, taking my time over it. I'd a gross of cheap machine-lace-edged hankies, nicely folded in tissue, and the trick was to tap some old girl's shoulder most politely, and say, "Ma'am, your bag's come open, did you know?"

"Gracious," she'd cry, "when did that happen?" and be all of a flutter, saying, "Thank you so much for telling me," and "I never noticed."

Of course she hadn't noticed because I'd flipped it open as she craned up at the cockatoo.

"Better look and see if everything's there," I'd say, looking around as if I expected to see two or three tiaras and a pearl necklace lying on the pavement.

"No," she says, "purse, comb, pins, peppermints—everything seems to be here. I am very much obliged to you, young man."

While she's in this happy and grateful mood, I sell her one of my lace-edged hankies to add tone to her collection of frippery. People will buy anything in the street, specially when they feel obliged, for five times the price they'd ever consider laying out in a shop, and in a couple of hours I'd got rid of fifty fourpenny hankies for half a crown apiece.

I wasn't really in it for business, just for pinmoney, and when I got up toward the racetrack, I eased off. For one thing, the last old diehard, after I'd sold her my story about Chantilly lace and she'd handed over her half-crown, disconcerted me by very deliberately flicking open the tiny handkerchief and blowing her nose on it, fixing me all the time over the top of it with a bright triangular blue eye like a flint arrowhead.

"Young man," she said, "you'll go far. Too far, if anything."

There I stood, rooted, unable to move out of the presence of that eye, until she dismissed me with a little nod, not unkindly.

So I strolled off and started paying attention to the runners. I made out with a couple of low-priced ones right away, so then I had a smoke and relaxed. No sense in hurrying a good chance. Mother always used to say, "Blow on your luck and give it a rub."

Crowds were still whirling up from the station, with whistles and paper snakes going full blast. It was a good day. You could smell the salt from the sea, five miles off.

I went and had a glass of stout and a sandwich at The New Pin, a chilly, smelly little place but nearest to the course, and then I strolled back, looking about, as I say, taking my time. Then, at three o'clock, I noticed an outsider at 100 to 1, Clever Cockatoo. That's for you, my boy, I thought, so I put a fiver on him. Silly thing to do I suppose, really, but I was feeling happy and relaxed and I knew it was my lucky day.

Clever Cockatoo strolled home by about five lengths.

In a way I was quite annoyed. I felt it had happened too early in the day. I knew if I had any sense I wouldn't bet any more, though it seemed a waste of the rest of the afternoon. Anyway, I thought, I'll give it a rest for a race or two, so I collected the takings and wandered off to a corner of the track where they'd got a little bit of a carnival going.

There were games and the usual sideshows, strong men, a snake charmer, bearded lady, Astounding Peep Show, some performing dogs. I watched the snake charmer, which was not a bad shilling's worth, though she was a skinny girl and the snakes definitely were not cobras.

Then I moved on to the last tent. In front of it was a notice that made me rub my eyes and look again, for it said, ADMISSION £5. Over that there was a picture of a naked girl standing still and staring straight ahead of her, crudely enough done, and, in larger letters; ELANA—THE GIRL IN THE BALL.

I stared at the chaps going in, and, sure enough, they did seem to be handing over fivers or grubby batches of notes. Well, I thought, this is putting it over on the grand scale, and

makes me look like an amateur. What persuades them to part
with their money?

There was nothing so startling about the notice, and I
wasn't going to be hurried into making a fool of myself just because I had all that money burning a hole in my pocket, so I
hung about and watched. After five minutes or so a hand came
out of the tent and reversed the notice so as to show the
words, FULL UP. Then some vaguely eastern-sounding music
began, plaintive and squeaky. Apart from that there was dead
silence from inside the tent—not a grunt, not a murmur.

The silence lasted for about ten minutes, and then the
music ended on a high, drawn-out quaver and, after a pause of
a moment or so, the chaps began coming out again. I studied
their faces. They certainly didn't look disappointed, or as if
they thought they'd been tricked; far from it. They were dis-
cussing eagerly, excitedly, among themselves, sometimes glancing back; but as soon as the last of them was out the tent flaps
were firmly laced together again.

"Is it good?" I asked an old fellow, military-looking
man.

"Remarkable," he said. "Quite remarkable. How the
devil did he get her in there? Go and see for yourself, young
feller."

That decided me and when the tent flaps were opened
once more I joined the stream of ingoing customers and
handed over my fiver to a giant of a man in a turban. We went
past him through a curtain, and you could hear a sort of sigh as
each man stepped in.

The inside of the tent was quite bare, except for a
roped-off square in the middle. Outside the rope was grass,
trodden into chalky dust by this time. The center square was
covered by one great piece of Indian carpet which was thin and

worn, but you could still see the original colors and patterns glowing in that queer, green, luminous light that you get inside a tent in daytime.

Each man as he came in made straight for the rope and leaned out over it, the later arrivals peeling off and working farther and farther around the square till the rope was completely lined with silent, staring faces.

Occasionally a man would murmur to his neighbor.

"Is she real?"

"Looks like it."

"Why don't she move then?"

"Dunno."

In the middle of the carpet was a clear glass ball, like the ones fishermen weight their nets with; only this one was perhaps three feet six in diameter, perfectly clear glass that looked no thicker than a brandy snifter. There was no visible mark or join on it, and yet inside sat a naked girl, quite still, but, so far as we could see, alive.

She was holding a bunch of spring flowers—narcissi, grape hyacinths, and so forth—and there was a whole mass of flower heads tumbled into the ball with her.

"She must be a waxwork," somebody said, and just after that the girl moved.

She had been looking down at the flowers she held, now she lifted up her eyes and gave us a clear, attentive look, unsmiling. She was dark-eyed, with a wide mouth and long blue-black hair that hung down her back to her waist. It had a ripple in it, and looked very soft, like dark feathers. The girl was slim and, so far as I could decide, not tall, perhaps five-foot two or three. As she sat, the top of the ball just cleared her head.

There was a lot of charm about that girl; she was the sort of girl you'd like to have come and sit herself down beside you on the top front seat of a double-decker bus on a fine spring day at the start of a twenty-mile journey. The only fault in her was that she never smiled, but then I daresay she couldn't be expected to feel much like smiling inside of a glass ball. Though if she was getting a half-share of the profits you'd think she might have felt inclined to smile at the thought of twenty five-pound notes standing around her and gazing at her so seriously.

In a moment the turbaned fellow came from his seat at the entrance, ducked under the rope, brisk and businesslike, and picked up the ball. He did it quite effortlessly, but you could see the muscles in his arms ripple. Holding it before him like a beachball he made the tour of the ring.

"You see, gentlemen," he said, "there is no deception about this. The girl is alive, the flowers are alive, and the ball is pure glass, unflawed. If I were to drop it, it would break. Tap it if you like."

Most of us did tap it, and it rang like glass all right.

"Now," said the man, "I shall show you some juggling."

There was a little portable phonograph in one corner of the ring, and he wound this up. It had a record already on it and in a moment the doleful squeaky music began and he started his act.

It was really dancing more than juggling. He postured about with the ball for a minute or two and then tossed it in the air. When he did that the flowers whirled up inside like those snowstorm paperweights, and then settled again as he caught it, some of them lying on the girl who was now curled up in a new position.

You could have heard twenty sighs as we all let out the breath we had been holding, and then he shifted the ball in his hands and tossed it up once more. That girl must have been

95

made of rubber; you'd have expected her to be black-and-blue, but I couldn't see a bruise on her. I daresay most of the audience had stiff necks next day, though, from following the ball in its flight.

Once or twice the man launched the ball toward the audience, and then dived after and caught it like a rugby player, just as they were ducking, or reaching up to finger it down. Inside the ball was like a kaleidoscope with the girl's white arms and legs at all angles and the flowers bursting upward like bees, and her black hair sprayed across it all.

Ten minutes lasted no time at all. The record came to an end; the man stopped his weaving around and put the ball carefully down in the middle of the carpet once more.

"You like it?" he said cheerfully, and there was a murmur of "Not half" from the chaps beginning reluctantly to file out into the daylight. The girl began calmly combing her hair with her fingers, shaking the flower heads down to the bottom of the ball, and straightening her bouquet.

I filed out with the rest and stood stupidly in the raw daylight, not knowing where to go or what to do. In the end I went down into the High Street and sold off the rest of my handkerchiefs, but it was really just to give my mind time to settle; I felt as if I had the girl and the flowers whirling about inside my head.

Then I went back and watched another performance. It was dark by now, the races were over, but the carnival was going full swing, and people were dancing in the street and up on the racetrack. There was a bonfire and some men had those torches they use for Guy Fawkes—metal holders with paraffin-soaked rags flaring in them—and were running about letting out whoops and scaring the women.

The tent was lit up by greenish flickering hurricane

lamps and the light reflected in the ball and in the girl's eyes was uncanny, inhuman—more like the light you see in a cat's eyes, caught in the headlights at night. The audience was tense, on edge—and very unwilling to go at the end of the performance. But the man in the turban shepherded them all out, shouting "Closing down, closing down now. No more tonight."

He caught hold of my arm as I edged between the flaps and said, "Wait." So I waited till the last man had gone grumbling out into the dark and said, "What is it?"

"You like this little show? It's a good little show, no?"

"Not bad," I said.

"You like to buy?"

"Why? You want to sell?"

"I must sell. I shoot a man in Chatham—see? Police after me. I am leaving tonight for France."

"How much?" I said.

"A thousand."

"Make it five hundred."

"O.K.," he said, "I have no time to argue."

All the time we were talking he had been changing out of his white rig and turban. I gave him the five hundred in notes and he left, blowing a kiss to the girl in the ball, and slipping out quickly between the tent flaps.

I stood holding onto the rope staring at her, and I must confess I felt a bit scared, didn't know what was going to happen next. This certainly was shaping out into a queer day, like a page torn out of a dream. I wondered what I ought to do with the girl—did I throw a rug over her for the night, like a canary? Or what?

Then I noticed that she was making signs to me, pointing over to one corner of the tent. I looked where she was pointing and saw a hammer. When I held it up, she nodded and began another pantomime. It took me a bit of time to get her drift, but at last I realized that she meant me to break the ball. That shook me a bit, because if the ball was broken, where was my show? But then I supposed she couldn't spend her life in the ball; she had to eat. I reckoned there must be a supply of balls somewhere behind the scenes.

So I broke the ball with the hammer.

I was rather startled when I discovered that she was French, couldn't speak a word of English. Her name was Marie-Laine. While she was slipping on the navy-blue dress that lay in another corner of the tent and twisting her hair into a chignon, I pointed to the bits of broken glass ball and said, "Où sont les autres?"

She flung out her hands, shrugged, and made a noise like Pfui.

"Alors, comment construire . . . ?" My French was pretty rusty, and I labored over the point I was trying to make: how the devil do we get you into another ball!

"Sais pas, moi," she said.

I gave it up for the time and, as I was pretty hungry and I reckoned she must be too, tucked my arm into hers and took her down for a steak and chips at The Anchor Hotel.

It was a funny sort of meal. She certainly was hungry—she waded into that steak, chattering away nineteen-to-the-dozen all the time in French about her stamp album which she had brought with her tucked under her other arm. She was mad about stamps. The waiter who served us got all excited and before the end of the meal she had him swapping a Suid-Afrika for a Togoland. All the men in the room were watching her with absolute fascination, she was so pretty and so much alive. She had the sort of velvety darkness and lightness of a kitten as she sat waving her expressive hands about and showing me her *timbres*.

"Come on," I said at last, "*marchons*. Time to go."

And we strolled back up the High Street which was empty by now, peaceful and starlit.

In the morning she was gone, with her stamp album and the rest of my money, leaving me only the tent, which was hired anyway as I soon discovered, and the memory of the sweetest night that two people ever spent on a faded old Indian carpet.

# Summer by the Sea

*How hot it was that* summer, and how it rained; the small wooden box of a house on the shingle bank seemed always crushed into itself with the heat and with the downpour which fell, sometimes for days together, out of a windless sky. The sea at these times became a flattened surface, and the shingle bank tapered to a point in either direction, the town vanishing altogether behind a gray curtain of rain.

Rue Penniston sat, during such a storm, in the small front room. It was evening, she was on the couch with her feet up; a detective novel and a history of mysticism lay beside her, but she was not reading. She looked pinched and faded, as if the rain and heat had washed the goodness out of her.

After a while her face assumed a listening expression and she called out, "Paul, is that you?" The back door clicked and there came the sound of a tap running. Presently a man appeared, rubbing his hair dry with a towel; he wore a dark London suit but had left his shoes and dispatch case in the bathroom.

"No sailing tonight," he said, putting down the towel and revealing a raspberry pink, plump face and a mop of frizzy black hair. "There's not a breath of wind."

"You'll find the cold meat and salad in the larder," she said without moving. "Have you seen the child anywhere?"

"Probably stayed at school. His raincoat's hanging in the entry so he'd have nothing to come home in."

"Oh well, he'll be able to borrow something." Her tone had no interest in it, and she picked up her book and began to read, while Paul put on a pair of tennis shoes, took the cold meat into the dining room, and began to eat his supper over the evening paper.

"Here he is," he remarked presently, as a dripping figure crunched over the shingle and past the window. The front door opened and a small boy came in. His soaked shirt and shorts clung to him and a pool formed around him on the rush matting.

"You seem to be very wet," said Rue.

"I waited for it to stop, but it didn't. I expect I might as well change into my pajamas and dressing gown, mightn't I?"

"If you want to."

"I'll dry Pickwick first, though."

Going through to the back he let in a draggled white

101

dog and began rubbing it in a businesslike way. Then he took from his school satchel a tin of dog food, opened it, and put some on a plate.

"See he doesn't get hold of the tin," he said to Paul, and went upstairs.

"I forgot to get any cornflakes, so you'll have to have bread and butter," Rue called as he came down again.

"Doesn't matter."

When he had cut some bread he said through the open door:

"Aunt Rue."

"Well?"

"Can I have a Bible? Madame said she'd get me one like hers."

"What do you want a Bible for? Are you religious?"

"Oh, it's a lovely one, with real marble covers and maps and pictures and all the Apocrypha in it too."

"What are the marble covers for? Surely that must make it very heavy?"

"To keep off bullets, of course," said Paul, who had finished his paper. "An improvement on the usual paperback edition."

"Is Mrs. Saunders making you a present of it?"

"Oh, I expect so."

"It sounds most unlikely to me."

"I'll call in tomorrow on my way to the station, if you like, and discuss the matter," said Paul, getting up and stretching. Rue looked at him skeptically.

"Thank you, Uncle Paul."

"It's time you went to bed. And don't call me Uncle. Is that dog dry?"

The dog and child went upstairs to bed, and Paul strolled into the front room.

"How's the heart tonight?" he asked.

"Bad," she said listlessly. "This weather's doing it no good."

"We could move from here if you liked."

"We've taken the house for the summer, we may as well stay. I daresay it'll last my time. Besides I might lose you in the move."

"Oh no. I don't mind staying around," he said easily. "Like me to get old Jakes in?"

"What's the use? He'd only give me another injection. I'd much better die and get it over."

He shrugged his shoulders and remarked, "The State pays for it either way. Well, if there's nothing I can do I'll go off to the yacht club and get a game of billiards."

"All right. I shan't sit up for you."

"I'll try not to wake you when I come in."

"Don't worry. I shan't be asleep."

As he went out she fixed on his back a look of love so unmixed with any kindly emotions that it seemed hardly human.

In the mornings Rue lay in bed late, while Paul and the child got up at different times, ate their breakfasts independently, and went off to school and office. Next day, however, the child saw Paul standing on the school porch, talking to old Mrs. Saunders, who preferred to be called Madame. The dog Pickwick was tied up there, as Rue refused to have him in the house during the day. From time to time Paul stooped and patted him.

At eleven o'clock Madame called the child over to her.

103

"I am sorry to say that your uncle considers fifteen shillings too much to pay for a Bible."

"Oh." He was not much disappointed. The desire for the Bible had been artificially stimulated by Madame herself, and he was already thinking of other things.

"What a charming man your uncle is. One would hardly know that he was an Australian from his accent."

"He's not my uncle."

Madame threw him a sharp look and said, "Run along now, and please stop that dog barking."

In the evening, as the child had again left his raincoat at home, Paul strolled along with it to fetch him. As he entered the small wooden building he heard the voices of Mrs. Saunders and the assistant mistress.

"Two weeks, Miss Lang, seems very insufficient notice to give for a day off. How do you suppose I can replace you?"

"I'm sorry, Madame," replied Miss Lang humbly. "My sister only decided on her wedding date two days ago."

"I'm afraid it's out of the question that you should go. Your sister should have decided sooner. And while we are on the subject, Miss Lang, I feel I should say a word about your work, which has not been at all satisfactory lately."

At this moment the old lady turned and caught sight of Paul.

"Ah, Mr.," she said smiling. "Come to find your little nephew? I believe you will discover him in the inner room."

Paul found the child sitting on the floor with the white dog, reading old numbers from the *Children's Newspaper*. Madame smiled again as they came out.

"We find this a good time to discuss together our little

problems in curriculum and management," she said. But Paul was looking at Miss Lang, who stood by a cupboard tidying some books and papers. Her childish pink face was flushed as if she had been crying. Madame raised her eyebrows, and standing up, began to arrange her purple draperies for departure.

About a month later Rue looked up when Paul came home from one of his late evenings and inquired:

"How's the charming Miss Lang?"

"Oh, I shouldn't say she was charming, should you?"

"She must have some attractions, surely?"

Paul smiled deprecatingly and said, "I've brought you a new book."

"Yes, and what have you done with my turquoise ring?"

"Sold it to pay the light bill—after all, you won't need it much longer, and it's too large for you now."

"You brute," said Rue, but she spoke without indignation. Indeed, she was pleased if anything, and looked almost affectionately at him.

"If you don't want me to sell things you shouldn't leave them lying about," he said calmly.

"You sold the child's model airplane last week, didn't you?"

"He was tired of it. Besides, I deserve something for looking after him, which I do much better than you. All the time he's been here I don't believe you've cooked him a single meal."

"That was the understanding. I told Helen I couldn't look after him if he came."

"Oh well," said Paul yawning. "It's not my affair. I'm going to bed."

"I'll stay down here. I don't want to be disturbed."

"All right. Got your pills? Drink of water? Then good night."

"Miss Lang left today," said the child one evening.

Rue looked up from her couch.

"Oh really? Why?"

"I don't exactly know. She was crying like anything, and Madame said she wouldn't have any sluts in her school."

"And what did you think?"

"Oh, nothing," he said indifferently. "She wasn't bad, but she was a bit silly, sometimes."

"Don't you take an interest?" Rue asked Paul.

"People should be able to take care of themselves," he replied, without raising his eyes from the evening paper. She smiled faintly.

"Have you seen the new dog leash I got yesterday, Aunt Rue?" said the child. "I think I left it on the table this morning."

"No, I haven't seen it," she said, turning back to her book. The child glanced in a troubled way at Paul, who was looking out of the window with a vague expression. He said nothing, but started upstairs to bed.

"I expect you dropped it on the way to school," Rue called after him.

Madame always used purple ink, and took great pride in her handwriting, which was rather flamboyant. She was putting in the place names on a map of St. Paul's journeys next day when the child, glancing out of the window in bored indifference, saw his dog Pickwick run out into the main road, dangling a length of broken leash. A car full of people came quickly around the corner, there was a jolt, the car slewed around at an angle but recovered itself and went on, and a man stepped off the pavement and picked a white, inert bundle from the road. He shook his fist after the car, which was now out of sight.

"Oh, Pickwick—" exclaimed the child, his eyes as black as coals.

"What's the matter," said Madame absently, writing in Antioch. "Sit down, I haven't finished."

"It's Pickwick, my dog. He's been run over."

"I noticed this morning that his leash was disgracefully worn. You should have tied him up more securely. No, sit down, I can't let you out now."

"But I must go out," he said in agony. "He may be hurt or dying, and he'll want me."

"For the last time, must I tell you to sit down," said Madame coldly. She glanced around. "That man will take him to the police station, I expect—you may go down there and inquire when school is over. It is entirely your own fault for not taking better care of the dog."

After school the child ran to the police station, but the accident had not been reported there, and no one knew who had carried off Pickwick. He went home, but Rue had heard nothing.

However next morning a man came around with Pickwick's body and explained that the dog had died during the night.

"I didn't know whose he was but the missus said he belonged to the little boy here. Regular brutes those people were that run him over; tourists of course. Shouldn't be allowed on the road, that sort."

"Oh, well, I daresay they were in a hurry," said Rue. She

thanked him, and then took the unusual step, for her, of going down to the school.

"I should like to take my nephew home," she said briefly to Madame. "His dog has been killed."

"I am aware of that. It hardly seems a sufficient reason for a day's holiday."

"I doubt if he is paying much attention to his lessons at the moment," said Rue coldly. She found the child in the inner room, pale and sodden. "Come along," she said, and led him out, darting one sharp glance at Miss Lang's successor, a plain, spectacled young woman.

"He's dead," she told the child when they were outside. "He died at once. Don't cry so, it all happened very quickly."

She said nothing further, but took him home and let him cry himself out.

"I can't really sympathize," she explained seriously then, "because I'm so near dying myself that I'm pretty well dried up inside. You'll just have to get through it. But we can give him a funeral. Would you like to bury him at sea?"

The child nodded. She found an old flatiron, which they tied to Pickwick's paws, and then between them they dragged the rowboat down the shingle.

"This will probably kill me," said Rue, as she rowed out. "I hope you can manage the boat well enough to get back if I collapse."

But she did not collapse, though she went white around the lips, and when Paul came back in the evening he was told the story.

"You'll probably have the sanitary authorities after you," he said drily. Then he dug in his pocket and found a pound note. "There, you'd better buy yourself a puppy at the pet shop."

"I don't want another dog now."

Paul tucked the note into his hand.

"You'd much better spend it right away, otherwise I shall probably take it back to pay the grocer's bill. Come along, we'll go to the pictures. I haven't had a night out for a long time. You'll be all right, Rue, won't you? Got your pills?"

Rue nodded; she was too tired to speak, and lay back against her cushions watching them as they went out.

# Minette

The largest thing in the tiny kitchen was the refrigerator, and the next largest was Harry Makins the bus conductor, sitting in the zinc bathtub, steam-wreathed and pink, with the thick undergrowth on his chest all out of curl, singing softly to himself as he cut his toenails in a leisurely manner and placed the trimmings in a china dish ornamented with rosebuds.

His bath stood in front of the grate, and above him, ranged on red velvet, pictures of Makins grandparents and second cousins smiled stiff tallowy smiles. A kettle hummed on the stove.

Mr. Makins deposited the last toenail and was on the

point of a careful emergence from the bath when footsteps pattered outside the back door and his wife's voice called, "It's only me, Harry. Wait till you see what Susie's given us."

Mr. Makins rose with dignity from the steamy water and draped himself in a towel. He was a square-faced, hairy, stocky man who had been in the navy for thirty years and still wore his British Transport uniform trousers as if they were bell-bottoms.

"Well?" he said admonishingly. "What's that scatty sister of yours come up with now?"

Mrs. Makins hung up her coat and scanned herself briefly in the mirror. Years of keeping her complexion nice for Harry on his leaves had left her with gray-pink cheeks, hollow, but soft and smooth as well-rolled dough. A pair of eyes as uncomprehendingly sad as a lemur's stared briefly back at her before she stepped into the passage outside and reappeared with a large carton. When she put it down on the table, a loud sweet chirrup came suddenly and startlingly from inside it.

"Come on, get some clothes over your great self and you can see what's in it," she scolded. "Standing about in the kitchen mother-naked! And it's a female too," she added obscurely.

A female? Her husband directed a suspicious stare at the box before taking his conductor's uniform, which had been warming in front of the grate, and stumping off regretfully to the cold upstairs.

When he came down the carton had gone. A fine large birdcage hung on the wall; in it, silent now but sharply, observantly turning its head from side to side, perched a small yellow bird.

Pleased, eager, tremulous, Mrs. Makins stood beside the cage.

111

# THE GREEN FLASH

"There! Isn't she lovely! See her little feet? See her bright eyes? And guess what Susie's taught her to say! Come on, my precious," she adjured the bird. "Say what Auntie Susie taught you. Sweet, sweetums, then!"

Mr. Makins was affronted. A childless man, he was unaccustomed to babytalk, and he found it silly. Worse was to come. The canary suddenly put its head on one side and in a hoarse, sweet voice, like that of some grotesque tiny mannikin, chirped out, "Hullo, Harry Makins!"

"There!" said Lil fondly. "Anniversary present for us. Isn't she sweet! Isn't she a duck?"

Harry was still standing and staring at the cage without a word. Slowly an anxious uncertain expression began to grow in Lil's eyes. "You do like it, don't you, love?" she asked.

"Of course I do," said Harry hastily and loyally. He put an arm around her shoulders. "Smashing present. Whatever will Susie think of next?"

"Hullo, Harry Makins!" the canary sang out again, strident and sweet as a carillon.

"Will it do that all day long?" said Harry uneasily.

"I shouldn't wonder. When it gets used to us. It'll be company for me when you're off on the buses."

"Of course it will," said Harry, guilty in his relief at the thought of escaping from the overbearing chirrup into his single-decker. "Course it will, dear."

Harry always came in from morning shift at half past one. He was a strict teetotaller and never lingered at the pub on his way home. In a few days, however, he found himself envying the other men, loitering at the door of the White Rose to exchange a last word before entering his kitchen—which resounded with sweet shrill squawks like tropical dawn on the films, and Lil's silly phrases of endearment.

112

## Minette

Only during the afternoon was there a bit of peace. Lil always slept on her bed for two hours after dinner, and Harry either accompanied her upstairs and lay companionably reading beside her, or, on a fine day, rocked and smoked outside the back door. The canary's cage was covered with a blue cloth and gave out no sound save a subdued scraping and twittering until five o'clock when Mrs. Makins came downstairs to get the tea and send her husband off on his evening shift.

Mr. Makins was a great reader. While Lil snored and dreamed under the white counterpane in the afternoon sun, his library books took him far away, buffeting over strange seas, wading desert sands, or into the glimmering reaches of the past. He was particularly fond of historical romances, and always asked Lil, who did the choosing at the public library, to get him something with swords in it if she could. At the first "On guard!" Mr. Makins's spirit would spring erect as quivering steel.

"Nice book?" Lil asked, and moved yawning past him to put on the kettle.

"Not so bad. No swords yet, but it's historical. Real people. Charles the First and that lot."

"What, him who had his head cut off?" she said idly.

"It's a bit sad," Mr. Makins muttered, more to himself than aloud. Rousing, he asked, "Did you have any dreams this afternoon?" He always asked this question at teatime.

"Oh yes. Yes, I did." Lil began to laugh, though her sad eyes preserved their questioning inwardness. "I dreamed that you fell in love. Regular head over heels with some young snip of a girl."

"Dreams go by opposites, they say," Harry remarked warily.

"Let's hope so. Something else there was too—" she

sought, frowning, in memory, her teacup balanced on the edge of her saucer. "Yes, that was it. Going to the White Rose, you were, for a bottle of brandy. *Brandy!*"

"Here, hold on, Lil," protested her husband. "Who d'you think you're dreaming about? What did I want the brandy for?"

"For her."

"Who?"

"This young girl. She was dying."

Harry held his breath. Then, making an effort, he said boldly, "The brandy soon put that right, I bet."

"You won't ever really bring home any brandy, will you, Harry? The very smell of the stuff turns me sick, right away."

"You know I wouldn't, you daft thing. Hey, look at the time, I must be off." Mr. Makins clapped his conductor's cap on his head, gave his wife a hasty kiss, and swung out of the door. But as he walked down the cobbled lane his face was creased with a preoccupied frown. Brandy, he thought. Falling in love with a young girl. What worse fortunes might Lil's dreams have in store for him?

The daily twittering irritation of the canary, and his wife's besotted fondness for it, were forgotten in this new anxiety. For Mr. Makins had long since discovered, though he never mentioned it to Lil, that anything she dreamed about him ultimately came to pass. Once he had had to live through months of sweating suspense until one of the old single-deckers crashed into the garage wall as she had dreamed that it would. With great difficulty, on the grounds that it would upset her to hear about it, Harry had persuaded his mates not to mention the near-accident to Lil; he trembled to think how she would worry if she realized her strange power of prognostication. He had managed to conceal the other odd scraps of dreams-come-true: the purse he found in the street, the letter from overseas, the time he cut himself on the chopper. Lil was nervous enough anyway—though she did seem happier with the canary in the house, seemed to be making a proper pet of it. Blasted bird!

Mr. Makins slapped his ticket punch irritably on the bus office counter. He wasn't even allowed to have his bath in the kitchen now, because Lil didn't think it was nice with the bird there, watching, and so he had to stagger upstairs to the bedroom with buckets full of water.

"It's no different from a child," he grumbled. "If we had a nipper you wouldn't mind him seeing me in the bath."

"Harry! How can you say such a thing!" Lil's eyes filled with tears and he felt bad; shouldn't have mentioned children.

The bird was allowed to flutter loose about the house, and Harry took a slightly wicked pleasure in teaching it to come when he whistled, and trying to persuade it to fly up to the bedroom when he was in the tub there. But as yet it had refused to come more than halfway up the stairs.

"Excursion this afternoon," grumbled Ted, his driver, coming up behind him. "Remember? Upham Park with a pack of Frenchies."

Harry's disgust was profound. Flaming Frenchies, he felt, were about as bad as nattering canaries. With stony disapproval he watched them all climb on to the bus—thirty silly girls, skirts far too short, cropped hair flying about their eyes, jabbering away nineteen-to-the-dozen. Why did they want to come to England anyway?

Resentfully he unwound an immense reel of tickets amid delighted squeaks and oh-la-la's; then hunched himself at the back of the bus, taking no further part in the business.

But when they came to Upham Park, and the French

115

girls had all scattered, waving their hands and calling to each other over the old Tudor house, Mr. Makins found the silence and the sunlight and the green splashes of trees against gray stone too productive of thought. He began to brood and remember, to think of old griefs, and of Lil's dreams, and of that perishing canary.

Presently, whistling, he climbed down from the bus, flipped a casual hand at Ted, who was smoking over an evening paper in the front seat, and strolled off to where they sold the tickets. Half a crown; there must be a lot to look at.

Peering into the cool gloom he found first a hall, with bits of armor and things in glass cases, then a huge oak staircase, then a room full of portraits. No one else was there, and he wandered around, staring at the varnished faces across which sunlight fell in golden lozenges, fetching out here a heavy-lidded seventeenth-century eye, there a proud mouth, there a hand drooping under lace ruffles.

One face particularly caught Harry's attention; that of a young girl with fair hair sleeked back into ringlets, a pointed chin, and wistful eyes. What was she looking at so sadly, so fixedly? He found himself turning, staring over his shoulder to follow the direction of her gaze. She seemed to be staring at a portrait of Charles II, black-haired and saturnine as any film star, with his deep-grooved cheeks.

And then Harry noticed that beneath the girl's portrait was a label which said,

MINETTE, YOUNGER SISTER OF CHARLES II

The name was familiar from his reading. But why should she watch her elder brother so wistfully? Left out, perhaps, thought Harry—for Charles's eyes, sidelong, were full on Louise de Keroualle who smiled along the wall to his right.

"It's no good, Minette," Harry found himself whispering, almost aloud. "He won't play with you just now." But the expression in her eyes was so forlorn that, absurdly, he felt a great choking lump in his throat. He wanted to say, Never mind, dearie, tell Father all about it. Father'll help. Which was strange for he had never felt like a parent before. But then she, Minette, poor girl, had hardly had a father.

"Going clean daft," Harry admonished himself, and turned to leave, taking a last look at the sumptuous oak paneling, the gilt fittings, the stillness and splendor. A grand place to live—if you weren't shut in there.

A couple of French girls hurried past him, twittering. "Dépêche-toi, alors! On s'en va, tout de suite . . ."

He had better hurry too. But he lingered a moment longer and saw another of the girls run in and pause before the portrait of Minette. Something arrested and birdlike about her appearance caught his eye; he looked again and saw that she was using the portrait as if it were a mirror, setting her ringlets straight, smoothing the sleek hair above her brows. And she might have been the portrait's twin!

He felt impelled to speak.

"Could—could you tell me the time, miss?" he asked.

She turned, and at once he knew who she was. Recognition flowed between them. "You're prettier than the portrait," he said.

She smiled a little, spreading her hands. "You are so kind! Alas, I cannot tell you the time. I have no clock." She had a charming slight accent.

"It doesn't matter," Mr. Makins said. "Perhaps—perhaps there is something I could do for you?" They looked at each other: a long, candid look, that of old friends, or young lovers.

She said, "Could you, perhaps, come to see me? I am a little lonely here."

"I'll come whenever I can," Mr. Makins promised.

She smiled again, raised her hand in a graceful, accomplished gesture, and moved through a door into the next room. Slowly he walked in the other direction. Even now he could not believe what had happened. When he reached the bus he counted the chattering French cargo, all thirty of them, on board again. But nowhere among them was a small, slight girl with fair ringlets.

And then he really knew, and his heart began to ache.

At home, the kitchen was unwontedly dark. He found Lil in the little-used front room, crying by the photograph of their Emmy, who had died at six weeks.

"What's the matter, love?" he said anxiously. "Not feeling bad, are you?"

"It's not me, Harry, it's the bird. She's had a queer turn. Oh, I know you don't set so much store by her as I do. I just don't know what I'll do if that bird dies."

Now Harry realized why the house seemed so queerly silent. He carefully inspected the bird, lying with closed eyes and heaving tiny chest in a cardboard box lined with cotton wool.

"What she wants is a drop of brandy," he said at length. "That might do the trick. Don't cry, Lil. I'll pop around and get some. And if it doesn't help her, well, I promise I'll get you another bird. I believe I should miss her racket about the place, and that's a fact."

Lil gave him a watery smile as he found a coffee essence bottle and went softly out of the back door.

The brandy did the trick. Not all at once; but after three or four drops had been trickled, at half-hourly intervals, down the canary's throat, she suddenly opened one bright eye and fixed a strangely familiar look on Mr. Makins, standing anxiously by her with the dropper in his hand.

"I think she'll be okay now," he said, breathing heavily with relief.

"Oh, Harry! Clever boy! Isn't she a little duck!" Lil said softly, looking down at the yellow bird stirring gently in her box.

"Well, I'll go and have a bath," Harry said, sighing. He hoped that Lil would suggest he could have it in the kitchen, but she did not; only helped him carry up the water, and then returned to her rapt contemplation of the reviving bird.

Presently—"She's flying again, Harry!" she called up the stairs.

"Smashing." Harry rather gloomily soaped his chest. He felt flat, and horribly sad, as if some wonderful occurrence had passed him by. I must have dreamed it, he thought. Stopped in the bus, very likely, and dreamed the whole thing.

Suddenly he heard a flirt of wings, saw a flash of yellow, and the canary was in the room with him. A tap, the faintest scrape of claws on metal, and she was perching on the zinc bath handle, fixedly regarding him. He held his breath. He hardly dared move, so strange, so recognizing was the look she gave him from her bright eye.

"Well I'm danged!" he whispered.

And the canary whispered back, no louder than the rustle of a heartbeat, "Hullo, Harry Makins!"

# Dead Language Master

Mr. Fletcher taught
us Latin. He was the shape of a domino. No, that's wrong, because he wasn't square; he looked as if he had been cut out of
a domino. He had shape but no depth, you felt he could have
slipped through the crack at the hinge of a door if he'd gone
sideways. Though I daresay if he'd really been able to do that
he would have made more use of the faculty; he was great on
stealing quietly along a passage and then opening the door very
fast to see what we were all up to; he used to drift about silently like an old ghost, but if you had a keen sense of smell
you always had advance warning of his arrival because of the
capsule of stale cigarette smoke that he moved about in. He

## Dead Language Master

smoked nonstop; he used a holder, but even so his fingers were yellow up to the knuckles and so were his teeth when he bared them in a horse-grin. He had dusty black hair that hung in a lank flop over his big square forehead, and his feet were enormous; they curved as he put them down like a duck's flippers, which, I suppose, was why he could move so quietly. Even his car was quiet; it was a huge old German thing, we used to call it his Strudel, gunmetal gray, and he kept it polished and serviced to the last degree. He loved that car. The way it whispered in and out of the schoolyard, it was a wonder he hadn't run anyone down yet, and everyone thought he would sooner or later, as he was very shortsighted and wouldn't wear glasses. If someone kicked up a disturbance at the back of the classroom he'd first screw up his eyes and stick his head out, so that he looked like a snake, weaving his head about to try and focus on the guy who was making the row; then he'd start slowly down the aisle, thrusting his face between each line of desks; I can tell you it was quite an unnerving performance.

He seemed ageless; I suppose he might have been in his sixties but you couldn't be sure. He used to go to Germany every holiday and he had this dog Heinkel, a dachshund. Heinkel looked older than his master, he was wheezy and rheumaticky, blind in one eye and had a wooden leg; I'm not kidding; he'd had to have a front foot amputated for some reason, and had this little sort of stilt strapped on so that he could hobble slowly about. He didn't bother much, though; sat in the car most of the time, dozing and waiting for the day's lessons to finish.

None of our lot cared greatly for Latin, we didn't see the point of it, so we didn't have much in common with old Fletcher. We thought he was a funny old coot, a total square—he used words like "topping" and "ripping" which he must have picked out of the *Boy's Own Paper* in the nineteen-tens. He was dead keen on his subject and would have taught it quite well if anyone had been interested; the only time you saw a wintry smile light up his yellow face was when he was pointing out the beauties of some construction in Livy or Horace. Personally I don't mind, if you've got to do a thing you might as well do it decently, but a lot of the guys thought he was a dead bore. That was as far as it went until Pridd arrived, and till Fletcher became our form master.

Pridd's father was the new manager of the new supermarket; the family had just come to live in the town. Pridd was a big lumping boy, with a small head perched on no neck, and small knowing Chinese eyes. He liked math, but every other subject bored him; he used to sit at the back of the room reading Hotcha inside his exercise book or filing down a bit of brass curtainrod to shoot peas through. He detested Latin; couldn't see the point of it.

"I'm going to help my dad in the shop as soon as I get out of here," he said, "so what the hell's the use of a lot of crummy Caesar and Virgil? Latin's a dead language, who cares about its flipping principal parts? Principal parts! I'll bet old Fletcher hasn't even—" and he added something obscene; Pridd was very foul-mouthed and thought himself highly witty, but personally I considered him an utter thick; he used to barge straight into girls on purpose with his one hundred forty pounds of misdirected energy, specially if they were trying to carry home a bowl of custard or jelly they'd made in Home Ec. His favorite idea of a joke was flicking glue onto girls' hair or pouring a bottleful of ink into somebody's desk when they weren't looking.

It was Pridd who christened Fletcher the Dead Lan-

## Dead Language Master

guage Master. "Look out, here's the D.L.M." he'd call in a piercing whisper, just loud enough to be heard, as Fletcher creaked in. Somehow the name stuck; it seemed gloomily appropriate to the poor old boy.

When Fletcher became our form master we suddenly realized that, instead of seeing him three times a week in Latin periods, we were stuck with him nearly all the time. He used to drift around like a moth between periods to see what we were up to, and there was nearly always trouble.

"Nyaaah," he always began his sentences. "Nyaaah, Pridd, what are you doing up on that windowsill?" He had a nasal, croaking voice like some rusty old bird.

"Nothing, sir," Pridd would answer innocently, dropping the paper waterbomb he'd just constructed onto some girl's head and sliding back into the room all in one movement.

"Nyaaah I don't really think that's so, Pridd, I'm afraid that means another visit to the headmaster."

Pridd scowled. We don't have beating at our school, the main punishment is Saturday detention, and after Fletcher had been with us for three weeks Pridd had piled up enough Saturdays to last him right through the term. This riled him, because on Saturdays he always put on a white overall and helped his dad in the shop, earning three or four quid a time.

"I'll get my own back on the old louse, you wait and see if I don't," he muttered.

He needn't have bothered. His mere presence in the class was revenge enough. From the day of his arrival our form began to go to pieces. Sometimes only the four guys in the front row were making any pretense of following the lesson; everyone else would be watching Pridd and snickering at his crazy antics.

123

"Fat woman going upstairs," he'd say, puffing out each cheek alternately, squinting at us out of his mud-colored slit eyes. He'd buy plastic balloons and blow them up into rude shapes, or pass round pictures, or tell stories, of which he had an endless supply; most of them were just stupid but a few were funny. If he couldn't think of anything else to do, he'd pretend to accidentally knock all the books off his desk, or let fall the lid with an almighty crash, anything to create a distraction.

Most of the masters tolerated him to some degree, slapping him down when he really got them riled, but Fletcher frankly loathed him; the loathing was mutual, you could feel it between them, cold as liquid air. He really made Fletcher's life hell. The Latin lessons soon deteriorated into utter chaos; no one even tried to learn. You could hear the whistling and stamping and talk and laughter all the way along the passage. Fletcher began to look more and more wizened and yellow: scooped out and sunk in like some old vegetable marrow that's thrown out on the compost heap because it's past eating.

Funnily enough I forget what act of Pridd's it was that started the final buildup to crisis; maybe it was tying a black thread round Fletcher's inkwell and twitching it off his desk when he was translating; or it might have been the time when Pridd sawed half through the blackboard pegs so that the board crashed down on Fletcher's toe as soon as he started writing. Whatever the deed, it made Fletcher so mad that Saturday detention wasn't enough; he also canceled Pridd's permission to see the Fenner-Giugliani fight, and sent back the money to Pridd's father, and gave the ticket to another boy.

Pridd was absolutely savage with rage and disappointment; he'd been dead set on going to that fight. The school had had early privilege tickets, and it was now too late to get

124

another for love or money; nobody liked Pridd enough to give up a ticket, though he went around offering huge sums.

He began to plot revenge.

It was a tradition that Fletcher always took his form for a picnic to Butt Lake on the last Monday of the summer term, and at first Pridd had it planned that he'd somehow contrive to trip Fletcher and push him into the lake.

"I bet the old fool can't swim," he said. "Wouldn't it be a laugh to see him flapping about in the water, silly old goat? 'Nyaaah, save me, save me, oh, won't somebody please save me?' "

In the end, however, fate gave Pridd a different opportunity.

We were fooling about in the schoolyard early on Monday morning when we noticed a gaggle of boys around Fletcher's car, all staring in.

"Perhaps the old fool's left his wallet in the car," Pridd said hopefully. "Let's go and see."

It wasn't a wallet, though. It was the dog, Heinkel, stretched out limp and dead on the seat; he must have died of heart failure or old age almost as soon as his master had gone off and left him; not before it was time either, poor thing. Whenever my father saw him he used to say, "That dog ought to be put to sleep."

Pridd joined the group and stood staring at Heinkel with his hands in his pockets. Then he began to snigger.

"We can do something with this," he said. "This is luscious!" He tried the door handle.

Usually Fletcher locked his car doors, but today he hadn't. Pridd leaned in and picked up the dog.

"Keep around me, you lot," he said, "we don't want anyone to see us. Oh, won't the old D.L.M. be surprised!"

"Wotcher going to do, Priddy?" someone said.

"Wait and see," he said. I think he wasn't sure yet himself, as a matter of fact.

Suddenly I felt fed up with the whole business. I waited by the door as they went nudging and giggling up the stairs to our classroom. I was still hanging about, reading the notices in the hall, which I'd read hundreds of times before, when the school secretary came out. Her name's Miss Figgins, we call her Fig, of course; she's not a bad old thing, gray-haired and dumpy and motherly.

She looked in the car window and said, "Where's Heinkel? I promised to have him while Mr. Fletcher's in hospital."

"Hospital?" I said. "Is he going to hospital?"

"Oh dear," she said. "Slipped out. Shouldn't have mentioned it—he doesn't want it talked about. Don't pass it on, Gant, there's a good boy. I know you can be sensible if you choose."

"Okay," I said. "But you needn't bother about Heinkel, anyway. He's just died—the boys went to tell Mr. Fletcher."

"Oh dear," she said, "poor little thing. Mr. Fletcher will be upset. Not that it wasn't time, I must say. Well I suppose I needn't trouble, then."

When I got up to the classroom Fletcher had already arrived. He looked at me tiredly as I slid into my desk but didn't say anything. There was no sign of Heinkel, but the atmosphere in the room was electric; I looked about cautiously, wondering what Pridd had done with him. Then I noticed that everyone's attention was focused on the cupboard where Fletcher kept the books like Cicero and Ovid and Horace that weren't used every day; whenever Fletcher moved that way the tension in the class shot up a couple of degrees.

Fletcher wasn't getting out any books yet, though; he was returning homework, making sharp remarks as he passed each exercise book back to its owner.

When he'd returned the last one, he cleared his throat and addressed the whole form.

"Nyaaah! Attention, please. Attention!"

Pridd muttered something to his neighbor and a line of giggles shot along the back row like fire through dry grass. Someone spluttered, someone else coughed, and in a moment half the class were rocking about in hysterics, paying no attention to what Fletcher was trying to say.

I noticed Fletcher's hands were trembling. He looked about him two or three times, hurriedly, as if he hardly knew what he wanted, then snatched up the poker from the stove and banged on his table twice.

"Attention! I *will* have attention when I speak!"

A sort of silence fell. Only at the back Pridd was heard to mutter, "Dopey old nana," and someone let out a suppressed titter.

"Pridd!" Fletcher shouted. His chest heaved. He clutched the poker and started to step forward. We all waited breathlessly, wondering if Pridd had really gone too far this time and if Fletcher was going to bash him. But he didn't. He wiped his forehead with the back of his other hand and said, "I'm not going to give you a lesson today. I'm not going to teach you anymore. I'm leaving."

"Hooray," somebody muttered, just audibly.

"I'm leaving," Fletcher said, raising his voice. "And if you want to know why, it's because of you. It's because you've made my life an utter misery these last few terms with your stupid, senseless insubordination and your idiocy and your malevolence. You used to be a decent enough lot of boys. I

127

don't know what's come over you. I really don't. All I can say is, I'm sorry for the next man who tries to teach you Latin. You've finished me, and I hope you're proud of yourselves."

He stared at us, trembling, and we stared back at him. There were beads of sweat on his yellow forehead. He noticed he was still holding the poker and threw it down.

"I shan't be taking you on the usual picnic," he said. "Frankly, I've no wish to. Mr. Whitney will take you instead. Gant, you're head boy; here's ten pounds, you can buy some food with it."

"Oh gosh, thank you, sir," I said. I didn't want to take it, but he pushed it at me and went on speaking.

"I only hope that some day you'll come to understand the amount of suffering you caused. Maybe then you'll learn to behave like civilized human beings. That's all."

He turned and walked out of the door. Thunderstruck, we gaped after him. Then Pridd exclaimed,

"Christ, we've got to get the dog back into the car somehow!"

"Why?" someone said.

"Why, you nut? We don't want the dog in the cupboard for the next term, do we? Come on, pretend to take the old goat's Latin books down."

Fletcher was just getting into his car when half the class hurtled into the yard. He didn't seem worried about Heinkel— evidently assumed Miss Figgins had taken him. He gave us a short unsmiling look.

"What is it?"

"We just came down to say good-bye, sir, and thanks for the money," Pridd said unctuously. "You forgot your books, sir. Shall we put them in the trunk?"

"You needn't have bothered—I shan't want them

128

again." But Fletcher pressed the button that opened the luggage compartment. The flap swung back and down. Two or three boys clustered by the driving window and two or three more stood around Pridd as he took Heinkel from under his blazer. He sat his fat bottom on the lid and leaned far in, to stow the dog's body right at the back of the compartment. He was grinning again, his Chinese eyes were like slits, and it was plain that he was relishing the thought of Fletcher's reactions when he opened up to get out the books.

Fletcher started the engine and glanced into his rear-view mirror.

I'm not sure how it happened; evidently Fletcher couldn't see Pridd's head in the mirror, for he pressed the button to shut the trunk. The flap swung up, Pridd hastily and instinctively pulled his legs in, and, hey, presto! the trunk was shut, and he was inside it. Fletcher released the handbrake and the car shot silently forward, across the yard and out of the gate.

Somebody shouted, somebody waved frantically. But Fletcher took no notice—I suppose he thought we were just waving a ribald good-bye. Or did he know he had Pridd with him?

We shall never learn the answer to that, because Fletcher wasn't seen again. He didn't go to hospital. His car was found five days later, on a lonely stretch of coast, with Fletcher's clothes in a neat, folded pile on the driver's seat. Otherwise the car was empty, except for the contents of the trunk.

# The Windshield Weepers

All that country un-
dulates. It is like the movement of the conductor's baton in
the andante; you look away from the hillside you are standing
on, and see a procession of slow, gentle, orchard-covered folds
of land, which seem to be turning a little, sleepily, to expose
the longest possible stretch of flank to the warmth of the sun.
The horizon is never very far away. Beyond it, out of sight, the
true mountains begin, but their blue and snowy crags are hidden by the nearer ebb and flow.

It was a warm, lazy time.

Even though there were frosts at night, the mornings,

## The Windshield Weepers

after the first haze had dispersed, were mild with the stored heat of summer, and by half past nine the dew was gone from the trampled orchard grass; at first, water cascaded off the apple boughs and down our shirtsleeves as we picked, then the shirts dried, then suddenly we were too hot as the sun moved around the shoulder of the hill, and the grass became pounced with a random design of clothes, dropped as the wearers moved from one tree to another. Radio music spurted out, snatches of talk and laughter; the tractor moved tirelessly up and down the rows, collecting stacked trays of apples, leaving empties behind. The tall, white, triangular fruitpickers' ladders flashed like pylons through the dappled green and rust of the apple trees.

At night, in one's cabin, images of the day returned to closed eyelids, even brighter than reality; for the first fortnight I dreamed about trees and leaves and apples, the roughness of the branch, the palm-filling globe of the apple (picked with one quick upward thrust), the tilting sway of the ladder on hummocky ground. Then, by degrees, my dreams changed and began to deal with mountains, those unseen mountains over the edge of the rounded horizon; I pictured them sheathed in snow, hollowed by echoing caves, and split by ravines; every night I wandered among them searching fruitlessly for something unknown and tantalizing that always eluded me.

In the evenings, after picking was done, I tried to paint my dreamscapes, but they came through blurred and uncertain, maddening me by their crudity, by the way in which they overlapped and obscured the truth. Oil was wrong, so was watercolor; line was too insubstantial. I tried a woodcut (Mrs. Macarndoe had equipped the cabin with a princely supply of artists' tools) and it came nearer, but was still unsatisfactory. What could be the answer? I became more and more preoccu-

131

pied, almost unconscious of my surroundings all day, the flashing trees and the browning backs of the pickers, as I wrestled with my problem.

It was in such a state of mind that, one night, I went on gate-duty.

There was a perennial shortage of pickers, because Mrs. Macarndoe would employ none but personally selected applicants and, in these, ability to pick apples ranked as a very minor qualification; consequently it was a standing instruction that no one who passed the initial test was to be turned away, day or night. Suitable transients, if they arrived after Mrs. Macarndoe had retired, were given a night's lodging and breakfast to strengthen them for the forthcoming interview.

Gate-duty did not actually mean that one sat by the gate: merely, a private circuit connected one's cabin with the milk-and-apple vending machine that stood by the highway. If somebody put a coin in the slot this rang an alarm bell in the cabin and the circuit was opened up.

At about 2 A.M. the alarm rang. I was not asleep; I had been wandering restlessly about my cabin drinking black coffee and smoking. Sometimes I stared at my incomplete mountains, sometimes out of the window at the moon-drenched orchards. The night was very quiet. We were about a hundred and fifty miles from the nearest railway. Sometimes you could hear owls; sometimes just the thud of ripe apples falling.

When the bell rang, I was glad of the distraction. I took a notebook and pencil and sat down, expectant; the tape recorder clicked on.

I heard the machine go into its usual routine.

"Good evening, stranger." Mrs. Macarndoe's voice, nasal earnestness coming through the cordiality. "I hope you are enjoying our creamy milk. It is today's milking, from the famous Westover herd of purebred Jersey cows."

"Thanks," a young voice replied guardedly. Boy or girl? Too husky to say. "It'll do."

"Your apple," the machine pursued, "is the Westover Pearmain, a cross from Sturmer, Concerto, and Bramley. Would you care for another? Pull the handle on the left and a second apple will be delivered, free."

"Thanks again," the young voice said (was there a trace of irony?) "that's mighty kind of you, mister machine."

"When you taste your apple," the machine said, "you will notice that the flavor is a blend of grape, honey, and citron. No other apple has this unique, lyrical tang. Try a bite."

The crunch of an apple being bitten came clearly through the transmitter.

"Isn't that delicious!" the machine said.

"Maybe. Maybe, mister machine. But—you know—it seems like when you buy an apple you buy it to taste like an apple. No? I can eat an orange some other time. Or a grape. Still, I appreciate your thoughtfulness."

"I wonder what takes you traveling at night, stranger?" the machine said.

"I guess that's my business, machine, old buddy," the voice answered. "Though it's kind of you to inquire."

"I wonder if you are looking for a bed for the night? Or are in need of a job? We can always employ apple pickers if they have the special qualifications required by Westover Enterprises."

"And what qualifications would those be?" the young voice said cautiously.

"You are a night voyager, stranger. Perhaps you are

alone. Perhaps you prefer to avoid the common mass of humanity? I wonder if you are a poet or a painter? Or maybe you are a composer of music?"

"I'm afraid you're out of luck, machine-feller," the young voice said, sounding amused. "I'm not any of those things."

"Even if you are not a professional," the machine continued, unheeding, "is it possible that at some time or another you have written a poem? Painted a picture? Made up a song?"

"You surely do have some crazy ideas about what's necessary for apple-picking," the voice remarked. "If your pickers have to be budding Beethovens or Botticellis I suppose that explains why the flavor of your apples is so all-fired lyrical."

"Think!" the machine urged. "Take your time. If you have ever written a poem, perhaps you would care to recite it? When you are ready, press the handle on the right as an indication that you are about to begin." (This had the effect of sounding a buzzer, which was a signal to the man on night duty to have his critical faculties in readiness.)

"Oh, all right," the young voice said with a hint of weariness. "I guess I've walked about as far as I can make it tonight anyway; wouldn't say no to a bed, and a place to hole up for a day or two. I have written a song, as it happens. Shut your eyes, machine-feller, and take a deep breath."

There was a thud, as something was laid on the ground; then, unexpectedly, a twang of guitar strings.

The buzzer sounded, the guitar muttered out an odd little primitive tune, all on four notes, and the voice began to sing:

> Make sure there's plenty of ice cubes,
> Make sure there's plenty of gin,

## The Windshield Weepers

Bring olives along to the mountainside
Before we're fastened in.

And bring along the Queen of Hearts
And bring along the Knave
There'll be many an hour to while away
When we are in the cave—

And hold me tight and warmly,
O, put your arms around;
For the cold is bitter where we are going
So far beneath the ground.

There was a long silence. Then I unclenched my numb
fingers from the pencil I had been holding, opened my cabin
door, and ran downhill through the majestic pattern of black
and silver tree trunks to the orchard gate.

"Well?" the young voice was saying drily. "You seem at
a loss, mister machine? Does that earn me a bedticket?"

I came around the corner of the vending machine and
stopped abruptly. The girl turned and saw me.

"Hi, brother," she said. "Are you the owner of this one-
armed mouthpiece? I was wondering who made the next move.
Well? Do I qualify?"

"Oh yes," I said. "You qualify. Would you like to come
with me?"

"Nothing I'd like better." She hitched her guitar onto
her back again. She was wearing a plaid shirt, in what looked
like gaudy reds and greens—but the moonlight made it impossible to be certain of colors—over jeans. Besides the guitar she
carried only a small canvas bag, laced around the neck with
string. She was small and stockily built but walked with long
strides, easily keeping up as I led the way at a quick pace back

to my cabin. It was strictly forbidden for girls to enter men's cabins after 4 P.M. (apparently Mrs. Macarndoe could not conceive of immorality before that hour) and I ought to have taken her straight to the empty reception cabin, but I was curious about her.

"What would have happened if I hadn't qualified?" the girl asked, kicking an apple out of her path. It bounced, throwing up a black spurt of icy dew.

"I should have pressed a button and the machine would have gone into its B-routine: thanks for your interesting recital, sorry you haven't quite made the grade, best of luck on your journey, farewell, voyager."

"So it rested with you whether I was in or not."

"It rested with me. But only for tonight because I'm on duty. I don't own the place."

I held the door for her, and she stepped into my cabin. It was comfortable, if not tidy. A log fire smoldered on the hearth and the floor was covered with some kind of folk-weave matting that Mrs. Macarndoe had specially made for her at cut rates by poor Indians in lands afar.

I put more coffee in the percolator and asked her if she'd like to eat.

She shook her head. "Thanks. Your tutti-frutti apples have done me fine."

She squatted down by the hearth and warmed her hands. "Who does own the place then? And where do you come in?"

"Oh, I'm just one of the pickers. My name's Taylor."

"Taylor what? Or what Taylor?"

"Taylor Samuel."

"Mine's Sanchie."

In the dim glow of the lamp I saw that she was a little

older than I'd thought. Outside she'd seemed about seventeen, but now I reckoned she might be in her early twenties. She had straight hair, tied back, and an air of solemn inquiry. "Who's the boss?" she asked.

"Mrs. Macarndoe—she owns all the land around here."

"Why is she so sold on poets and painters?"

"Well," I said, thinking it sounded a little less mad in the moonlit small hours than at any other time, "she has this belief that sooner or later, if she hunts hard enough, she'll find the reincarnation of Coleridge."

"For Pete's sake! Why does she want to do that? You mean the guy who wrote *The Ancient Mariner*?"

"That's right."

"We did it when I was a kid at school. Something about an albatross. I always remember one bit," she said dreamily, staring into the fire. "Like one that on a lonesome road Doth walk in fear and dread. And something something turneth not his head; Because he knows a frightful fiend Doth close behind him tread."

She glanced back over her shoulder. I put another log on the fire and a flame leaped up, illuminating my pictures stacked against the wall.

"You paint these?"

"Yes." I passed her a cup of coffee. "Coleridge didn't only write *The Ancient Mariner*. He wrote another poem called *Kubla Khan*."

"And so?"

"He never finished it. He woke up from a drugged trance and wrote half of it down and then a person from Porlock came knocking at the door and broke his train of thought. When the person had gone he couldn't remember what he'd been going to say next."

Sanchie had slipped off the soaked canvas shoes she had been wearing. She wriggled her bare toes in the warmth of the fire. Her feet were hard and supple and calloused as if she went barefoot more often than not.

"I remember now," she said sleepily. "Coleridge was a junkie, wasn't he? It's a mug's game, though—you get so you can't coordinate. My grammaw used to smoke cactus—she was half Indian, she brought me up—on her good days it really lit her, I used to listen to her for hours—"

"What sort of things?"

"Oh, stories, songs, what she called her messages—but the bad days got worse and worse; I had to stay with her all the time because she was scared of things coming after her. I was happy for her when she died. She got into the old Ford one day and drove over a cliff. . . . So tell me more about this Macarndoe dame, why does she think Coleridge is going to be born again? Is she nuts or something?"

"I don't think so; she's just got this one fixed idea. Most people have at least one, don't they?"

"I guess maybe. Grammaw certainly did, she had an idea about windshield weepers."

"What were they?"

"Sign of death, she said. When someone was going to die, or when something bad was going to happen, she'd hear 'em sobbing and weeping as she drove along in her old car—sobbing and weeping around the windshield. She foretold a plenty deaths that way. People used to say she was a witch, and I guess they were right. In the end she said the windshield weepers were wailing for her death, and she might as well go. So she tied 'em into a little bag and gave it to me. . . . What happened to Mrs. Macarndoe?"

"She lost her husband in an air crash. That shook her

loose from life. So she bought this place—she's very rich—and runs it to provide jobs for hard-up young poets and painters; you do a bit of work and in return you get your food and bedding and all the materials you need."

"Sounds okay." For a few minutes Sanchie sat nibbling the tassel of her little bag and staring into the fire. I began to have the impression more and more strongly that she was afraid of something; that only half, or less than half of her attention was given to me and Mrs. Macarndoe. What was it, back there on the long moonlit road, that was so occupying her mind, that kept pulling her eyes uneasily to the door?

"D'you think she'll let me stay?" she roused herself at length to say. "It's nice and quiet here—off the beaten track."

I remembered what she'd said to the machine—*a place to hole-up for a day or two.* Why was she so anxious to hide?

"I guess she will. I liked that song you sang—have you any others?"

"Some. A few I made myself. Lots my grammaw used to sing."

She rose and stretched; picked up her guitar, ran an idle thumb over the strings. "I like your pictures, too," she remarked, strolling over to look at them. "They remind me."

"Of what?"

"Of where I was raised, way down in the mountains. *Wa-ay down in the mountains,*" she sang,

> "*Of South Carolina,*
> *We slinga de ink and*
> *Pusha da pen along . . .*"

"Sing something else, Sanchie."

She sang another song, about a forsaken maid on Bram-

ble Mountain, sad and haunting enough to make your heart
falter in its beat. Then, filled with compunction, I said I
supposed I ought to take her to her cabin, she ought to be getting some sleep.

"No, I'd rather stay here awhile," she said. "I guess I'm
not so sleepy. And I'm no great shakes at sleeping in the dark."
Her eyes started toward the door, and she brought them firmly
back.

"Tell me some more about this *Kubla Khan*," she said.
"Have you got the poem handy?"

I had Coleridge's *Collected Poems*, and I fetched them
out.

"Read it aloud, why don't you?" she said. "Mind if I
take off my shirt and dry it? It was pretty dank and misty back
there along the road."

She took off both shirt and jeans, hung them matter-of-
factly over the back of a chair, and curled up with her head on
a cushion. The mood of the night was by now so far removed
from reality that I did not feel surprised at finding myself reading *Kubla Khan* aloud to a naked girl by a blazing fire; it
seemed merely odd that I had never done so before.

> ". . . *A savage place, as holy and enchanted*
> *As e'er beneath a waning moon was haunted*
> *By woman wailing for her demon lover.*"

Sanchie made a slight movement. I stopped reading.

"Were you going to say something?"

"Nope." But I waited, and she said with a slight effort,
"Of course it might have been the other way around."

"What might have been the other way around?"

"Coleridge might have been writing about *himself*. And

140

his demon girl, who went away and left him with his poem only half finished."

"Perhaps. I hadn't thought of that. What were you really going to say, Sanchie?"

"Nothing else."

She looked up at me innocently. She had found my comb and was combing her fine, straight hair out in a fan, so that its darkness was fringed with gold in the firelight.

"Why do you keep looking at the door? Are you scared of something?"

She held my eyes with a show of bravado for a moment. "I'm not afraid of *anything!*" she boasted. Then she hid her face in her hands, strands of hair tangled in her fingers. "That's not true; well, you know it isn't. I'm afraid—I'm afraid of *him.*"

"Of him? Who? Who frightens you?"

"He comes out tonight, you see," she whispered.

"Out?"

"Of—of prison. He's a guy I used—used to be with. I think—I *know*—he'll be after me again. Well, he'll be angry with me. And—and he scares me to *death!*"

"What's his name?"

"Goliath."

Curiously, as she said the name, I had a vision of a face, dark and low-browed and dark-haired, with the strength and ferocity and sorrow of the big apes; it hung in the darkness between me and the girl for a moment and then receded into distance.

"But he won't find you here, Sanchie," I said. "After all, he can't get in, can he? Unless he's a poet or a painter."

Her face unfroze at that, and she began to laugh a little hysterically.

"No, of course you're right, he can't get *in*! That's a joke, isn't it? Poor old Goliath, he can't even answer the questions, he's too dumb, he can't get in! That's true, you see," she said, instantly sobering.

"What's true, Sanchie?"

"That he's dumb—literally. He can't *speak*. Not now." A silence, heavy with unspoken words, lay between us for a moment and then she added in a low voice, "Of course he *could* get in if he wanted to—Goliath could get in *anywhere*."

"He'd have to ring the bell, anyway, and we'd hear him. How's he coming, walk, hitch, car?"

"He drives."

"You'd hear the car. You'd have time to hide."

"I guess so." But she sounded unconvinced. "Never mind. Forget it. Read me the rest of the poem."

> "*. . . For he on honey-dew hath fed*
> *And drunk the milk of Paradise.*"

"That's what my grammaw used to say. She had a song that told the same thing, the song about the Far Mountains."

"Sing it."

She played a soft chord. As soon as she began to sing I knew I had heard the song before. While half my brain was acknowledging this, wondering where I had heard it, the other half had discovered with lightning certainty what was wrong with my pictures and how it could be put right. . . .

The song died away unfinished. Sanchie's eyes were riveted on the door, which was opening slowly; a wedge of shadow slid across the floor. It crept on till it reached Sanchie's bare foot.

# The Windshield Weepers

"So!" said Mrs. Macarndoe's voice. "This is how you repay my hospitality! With vice and fornication!"

She stepped into the room. She was a formidable figure —not tall, but gray and gothic, gimlet-eyed, her nose a flying buttress, every iron curl netted into place.

"No, that's not so, Mrs. Macarndoe," I protested. "We've been doing nothing wrong. Sanchie wanted to dry her clothes and I've been reading her *Kubla Khan*—"

"What sort of a fool do you take me for, young man? I am not quite so innocent as you suppose. I can only ask you to pack your things and leave immediately; I am appalled—appalled—to think what I have been cherishing under my— my——"

"Apron strings," I suggested angrily. "Look, all right, Mrs. Macarndoe, I'll go if I must. Though I promise you no impropriety of any kind has taken place. But let Sanchie stay! Wait till you've heard her sing, you'll see what I mean! . . . And she's scared, she needs somewhere to hide—"

"Let that—that hussy stay? Listen to her sing? A likely idea! Clear off!" she snapped at Sanchie, who, quite unembarrassed, was putting on her shirt. "I hate to think of my orchard harboring such—such *things* as you."

"Okay, okay," Sanchie said pacifically, "keep your hair on, you poor old nutcracker, I'm not an apple-weevil. I'm not going to steal your fruit. Thanks for the rest and the chat, anyway," she said to me.

"Wait, Sanchie," I said, "I've got to pack all my stuff into the jeep, you might as well hang on and get a ride—"

"She'll wait *outside* my gate if at all," Mrs. Macarndoe said, breathing very forcibly up and down her nostrils.

"Well, thanks, no, I guess I won't wait. I'd better not

ride with you," Sanchie said. She slung the guitar over her back and gave me a little nod, formal but friendly.

"Don't leave this." Mrs. Macarndoe whisked up the small canvas bag distastefully by one string and pushed it toward Sanchie, who drew breath in a sharp hiss. The bag pulled open slightly, but nothing spilled out, and Mrs. Macarndoe, pushing it into Sanchie's hand, insultingly held the door open and ushered her into the night. The sound of their feet died away over the crisp grass. In the distance I heard a car change gear on the long slope of road leading up to the orchard gate. Was it my imagination, or did I catch somewhere, far off, a faint sound of wailing?

The new day was gray, and muffled in thick mist, when Mrs. Macardoe reappeared and grimly supervised the final tidying-out of my cabin.

"Good-bye, Mrs. Macarndoe. Thanks for your help. I'm sorry it ended like this."

"Good-bye, young man. So am I."

"I'm leaving you my paintings as a gift. I think I know what I'm trying to do now."

But did I? Stuffing socks and handkerchiefs into a kitbag I wondered if that half-formed vision would stay with me, or had I to begin again from the bottom? If I had words I might be able to describe what I'd seen; but then I'm not a poet.

"I'm not very interested in your painting, Mr. Taylor, I'm afraid—now."

Isn't that just like a woman? I thought, trudging down to the shed where the jeep lived. My feet left black snail tracks in the gray rime. Perhaps, I thought, if I drove fast, I might catch up with Sanchie.

Old Tom, the regular gateman, had already hobbled on duty. He opened up, and I stopped to say good-bye.

# The Windshield Weepers

"Sad doings down in the valley yonder," he said, gesturing south. "Motor crash down the bottom of Helter-Skelter Hill."

"Anyone hurt?" I asked with an aching premonition.

"Killed. Young gal. Stranger in these parts."

"Was she carrying a guitar?"

He looked at me blankly. "I couldn't say. No, that I couldn't say. Car was a proper wreck."

"What about the driver?"

"Driver? There wasn't but her in the car. Nobody else . . ."

Five miles down the road I came to the scene of the crash; some bits of twisted metal, some skid marks on the road. A few locals were still standing thoughtfully by the wreckage.

"Funny she wasn't in the driver's seat," one of them said, evidently for the twentieth time. "And what made her skid? Warn't no reason to skid there."

The remains of a guitar lay on the grass but there was no sign of a small canvas bag. I drove on. There was nothing else to do.

> A damsel with a dulcimer
> In a vision once I saw:
> It was an Abyssinian maid
> And on her dulcimer she play'd
> Singing of Mount Abora. . . .

# The Green Flash

It is not always easy to find the person you have arranged to meet in a small country town; cars and lorries pass, people bob in and out of shops, humanity seethes like the scum on boiling marmalade; but there was no difficulty in finding Colonel Pevensey Jones.

First he shot out of a small door labeled Coal Order Office, with such violence that lumps of coal might have been expected to come whizzing out after him; next he pursued a traveling fish van vehemently down the main street and plunged about among its piles of pilchards, mounds of mackerel, and heaps of herring with an irresistible resemblance to a sea lion selecting its breakfast. Then, puffing a little, triumphant, laden with the fish and various other packages, he made for his tractor, which was parked outside the post office.

Paul Hansler, who had been watching his friend with affectionate amusement for the last five minutes, now stepped forward and greeted him.

"Ah, Hansler! How delightful to see you, my dear fellow. Here we are, then, splendid—I'll just tie the fish on here— they fell off going up Polwheal Hill last time, it's very steep— and the rest of the things can go under here. Now, is there room for you beside the steering wheel or would you rather go in the trailer with the pigs—it would mean sitting under the net, I'm afraid."

Hansler looked at the tiny trailer, hardly larger than a card table, in which four sizable gilts nosed each other under a protective net, and elected for the tractor.

"I'm so glad you were able to come," yelled the Colonel, as they shatteringly breasted the steep ascent out of the town, "because I've a problem that's right up your street."

Hansler by gestures indicated himself willing to help so far as lay within his power. It was impossible to conduct a conversation above the noise of the engine, and he relapsed into silence, gazing about him.

The morning was still young—he had come down by the night train—and a clear frosty light hung over the landscape. They had drawn away seaward from the town and climbed up onto one of the heights of the long escarpment that undulated slowly up from the valley to end in thousand-foot cliffs against the Atlantic. It was not exactly beautiful country, but satisfying to the eye, with its dry waves of land, broken here and there by a leaning spinney of beeches, blown eastward by the wind.

Presently Colonel Pevensey Jones drew up his tractor

outside a whitewashed cottage by one of the spinneys; it was solidly built, low, and seemed to cling to the ground. Daffodils were blowing wildly in the garden and from the outbuildings came gusts of piercing squeals and a strong smell of pigs.

"Haven't fed 'em yet today," grunted the Colonel. "Late, with meeting you and fetching the new gilts."

He unhitched the trailer and dexterously tipped the new pigs into a hurdled pen by the farm gate.

"You go in and meet Betty—shan't be long," he shouted over his shoulder and stumped off—a short, solid figure in his tweeds, with an air of goodwill and integrity that breathed from him strong as the smell of peppermint.

Hansler had never met the sister. He tapped on the door cautiously, but noticing with approval the brilliantly polished knocker, pink hyacinths and scarlet anemones by the wall, fresh cotton curtains blowing, and a general appearance of cleanliness and prosperity. He was glad to think that his friend was so well looked after.

The Colonel's sister, when she opened the door, was a slight shock. He knew, of course, that she was Elisabeth de Reszke, well-known cookery expert with a dozen books and countless articles to her name, but nevertheless he had expected in this rural setting something homely, like a feminine version of the Colonel.

Miss de Reszke was certainly the same build as her brother, and probably the same age, but there the resemblance ceased. He was like the casing of the horse-chestnut, rough, brown, and knobbly; but she was the highly polished chestnut itself. A sibilation of French adjectives swam into Hansler's mind: svelte, soignée, chic, suave—as he took in her elegantly curved black silk and pearls.

She was amiability itself, showed him to a delightful lit-

148

tle bedroom, indicated hot water; and then waved him back to a log fire and a fragrance of coffee.

"How good, how kind of you to come all this way to see us poor rustics," she said over the white bone-china coffee service.

"Oh, but it's the most enormous pleasure," he replied truly, glancing around the book-lined sitting room. Its uneven floor was covered with Persian carpets in beautiful faded pinks and blues. "The air down here is so wonderful too—really electrifying."

"Electrifying?" She turned her bright eyes on him. "You find it so? It brings out your inmost self? That is most interesting."

Yes, he discovered on reflection, that was precisely what he had meant. The air down here stimulated a part of him that he had thought long dead; the buried writer who, exiled from his own land and bereft of his own language, had sunk deeper and deeper into silence. In this clear air Hansler felt once more to take the manifold world and make it his by putting it on paper—the snatch of gulls whirling and looping in dispute over the plowed field, this archaic, lovely house hugging the wind-blown ground, the eyes of the woman opposite, intently watching him.

The moment drew out, and he could hear the muffled sputter as a piece of log broke off and fell into the ash, and the clock in the next room clearing its throat preparatory to striking. He could not withdraw his gaze from hers, and her eyes were as brilliant as drills, with a point of light in the center of each. Suddenly he remembered a phrase of a nursery tale— "What big eyes you have, Grandmamma!" "All the better to see you with, my dear!" "And what sharp *teeth* you have, Grandmamma!" "All the better . . ."

# THE GREEN FLASH

"You must be admiring my contact lenses," said Miss de Reszke. Without the slightest change of expression, the slight smile still curving up into her full cheek, she put her hand to her right eye and rapidly manipulated her fingers; there was a flash, as of a glistening teardrop, she held out her hand to him, and he saw something small and bright in the palm. Then, with an equally rapid movement, she slipped the lens back in again.

Hansler was speechless, but before it began to be noticeable there was a stamping and a clattering in the scullery as the Colonel came in, kicked off his muddy boots, and began to wash; then he appeared humming like a basket of bees.

"Shall we have lunch now, Betty?" he said, rubbing his hands above the fire. "I thought I'd take Paul up to Treloe this afternoon."

"Oh, it would be a waste of time to do that on such a fine day," she said smoothly. "I'll get out my car, and we'll go for a drive. You'd like that, Mr. Hansler?"

Paul felt a most uncommon attraction to this woman—whether from her bright eyes, her rapid, deft movements, or the urbane friendliness of her manners he could not analyze; it was akin to the feeling he had toward some smooth, glossy-coated animal, full of silent vitality—perhaps a cat? There was something highly charged about her; he thought that if he laid a finger on the black silk of her dress a spark would run up his arm.

Lunch was a delicious meal—quite disproportionately delicious, Paul thought, working his way through paté and salmi, soufflé and fruit salad with a dash of kirsch. But he remembered the twelve cookery books and acknowledged that Miss de Reszke had to expend her talent somehow.

"Don't you ever come up to town?" he asked.

# The Green Flash

"Very seldom—I hate hotels, and I hate going out in the evening. That's when I do all my writing, you see."

The Colonel had an air of dissatisfaction—he was picking at his food with an absent face, but Hansler had no clue to the cause of his mood.

They went for the promised drive, and Hansler abandoned himself to the enjoyment of sheer terror—Miss de Reszke was a skilful driver and slung her car through the narrow winding lanes at a speed that could have meant instant death at many a blind corner if they had met anything coming the other way—but fortunately they never did. Paul made no attempt to conceal his feelings and she laughed at him, her eyes and teeth flashing. The Colonel sat in the back, silent, preoccupied; once he leaned forward, looking into a field, and said, "Kelvin's got his boar, then."

"He's a brave man to keep it out—unless it's really savage," his sister said, turning her head for a brief glimpse. Two stone gateposts flashed up to them, and Hansler shut his eyes but she threaded them, apparently without the need for sight.

After the drive the Colonel took Hansler to see his pigs, which were housed in neat concrete compartments. Hansler admired the arrangements for mucking-out, for feeding by means of a traveling hopper, for watering from a gravity-fed trough.

"You never let them out, then?"

"Daren't, my dear fellow. Animals around here get savaged if they're let out."

"But by what?"

"Hard to say. Some beast, outsize badger or wildcat, maybe. There are a few in the British Isles still. And this is an odd countryside, you know—uncanny. Matter of fact the problem I want your opinion on is something along these lines."

"I can't deal with the supernatural, you know," Hansler replied doubtfully. "I'm a psychiatrist, not an exorcist. But of course I'll be glad to help in any way I can."

"My turn now," said Miss de Reszke, meeting him outside the piggery. "Come and see my collection of wishbones."

Hansler was puzzled, but obediently followed into the study, where, sure enough, she showed him a series of cases lined with indented blue velvet, which contained many hundreds of wishbones, scrupulously polished.

"Heavens! What a lot of chickens you must have roasted," he exclaimed.

"Yes, mustn't I?" she answered, with a gleaming smile.

"Each one cooked by a different recipe? Your brother is a lucky man."

"Oh, he's not very fond of elaborate cookery—he'd just as soon have cold beef."

Hansler yielded to an irresistible impulse to put his arms around her and run a hand down the smooth, black-silk curve of her back. It arched a little, under his hand, and she looked up at him but said nothing; only, her smile widened, just perceptibly. They stood together for a moment, and then she looked at her diamond watch and said in a matter-of-fact way:

"It's getting late. I must go and change."

"Paul?" called the Colonel from the kitchen. "Care to come and watch for the green flash? I always do—sort of habit one gets into."

"Yes of course. What is the green flash?" asked Paul, following him out of the back door.

"Up on here," the Colonel said, clambering with agility to the top of the stone-and-earth bank that ended his domain. From there they had a view of the folds of land interlacing away down to the cliffs, and the silver line of the sea beyond.

The wind had dropped, and the sun was on the point of setting; it was clear, and very cold.

"The green flash?" Colonel Jones went on, steadily watching the golden disc of the sun as it sank. "It's something that happens just after the sun goes down—a flash from the horizon. Don't know what causes it."

"Have you ever seen it?"

"No, never. But there's no harm in hoping, is there?"

The last sliver of brightness dropped from view without any revelation. Hansler shivered.

"Goose walking over your grave," remarked his friend. "Or more likely a fox or a wolf in this country. Come along in. A peg of whiskey will do us good before dinner."

To Hansler's surprise the table was set for two only, and a cold meal was laid out.

"Betty never has dinner," the Colonel explained, measuring whiskey into glasses. "Doing her writing in the evenings, you know, she likes to put in a good long spell without interruptions."

"Oh—when she said she was going to change, I thought she meant change for dinner." Hansler could not decide if he felt relieved or disappointed.

"Change into writing things, I daresay she meant."

The meal was rather silent, and soon over. Afterward the Colonel said:

"If you didn't mind going out again, we could drive up to Treloe and have coffee there."

Hansler said he would be delighted, and his host went to fetch the tractor. The noise it made in the evening hush was even more deafening.

"I'd borrow Betty's car," the Colonel shouted apologetically, "but I never disturb her while she's writing."

153

They rode inland up steep lanes to the moor, where furze-covered hills reared against the darkening sky. At the foot of a grassy track the Colonel stopped the tractor saying,

"We'll walk up and I'll tell you about Diana as we go along."

"What is Treloe? A village or a farm?"

"It's a farm—a smallholding. Diana is a girl who's recently moved to these parts, she hasn't been here long. I've been able to give her a bit of help and advice—it's lonely for her up there. She seemed happy enough at first, just managing to make ends meet, but now this trouble has come on her and it's not so easy."

"What trouble?" asked Hansler as the Colonel paused.

"Well—she's very much ashamed of it, of course, but it seems to be some kind of poltergeist. Things fly about, you know, and bump, and it's really damned inconvenient—one can't afford to have objects getting out of hand on a farm."

"I suppose not," Hansler replied moderately, watching the Colonel's worried expression as he considered the problems of his friend.

"Do you think you might be able to help her?"

"I shall have to see her first." Hansler's tone was decided. "Sometimes these things are caused by outside agents, sometimes not. It all depends on the person."

The Colonel nodded.

It was too dark, by the time they reached Treloe, for Hansler to receive anything but a vague impression of stone walls and some small low buildings clustered together. There was a fresh moorland smell, the chill of stone, and a powerful sense of antiquity; they had been climbing steadily and might easily have arrived at some druid ring or circle of monoliths on a summit of the moor. Hansler was not surprised, when the

# The Green Flash

Colonel tapped and opened a door, to find the flickering uncertainty of lamplight and the primitive smell of peat-smoke.

His eyes smarted, and for a moment he could not plainly see the girl who received them. When he did he was appalled at her gaunt, mournful beauty. She was tall, easily his own height, overtopping the stocky Colonel. She was thin to the point of emaciation. Her straight lips and square-boned face had an air of resolution that was belied by her eyes—haunted, desperate eyes that plucked at Hansler's sensibilities almost unbearably.

"Don't you find paraffin lamps rather dangerous with a poltergeist in the house?" he asked.

"They call it a boggart around here," replied Diana, pulling a tin coffeepot off the fire. "Yes, I do, but of course there's no electricity on the moor."

The coffee she gave them was black and bitter. The Colonel seemed to have fallen into a sort of still content as he sat sipping, though his eyes, when they rested on Diana, were anxious.

"Have you had much trouble today?" he asked.

"A couple of bricks fell out of the wall and broke the cream pans, and spoiled all the cream. The mirrors kept falling down—I haven't an unbroken one left in the house. I've stopped putting things on the shelves in the pantry because they always fall off. And all the books you lent me, which were on my bedside table, suddenly flew out of the window into the paddock. I'm afraid they got a bit wet."

"It doesn't matter."

Hansler looked around him expectantly, but nothing stirred.

"Things often seem to quiet down when I have visitors," Diana said.

"How old are you?" Hansler asked her abruptly.

"Thirty."

He nodded. "Aren't you afraid—all by yourself up here?"

"Oh no—I have a gun." He nodded again.

"But I haven't told you," she said to the Colonel. "I don't know if I shall be able to stay here. A committee is coming to inspect my farm tomorrow, because they say I'm not working it properly, and I may have to quit."

"But they can't do that!" said the Colonel furiously. "What's the trouble?"

"It's drainage—I've put in a lot of pipes, but they always break. And my milk production is terribly low because such a lot gets spoiled. If I have to leave here, I don't know what I shall do."

Her tone was despairing.

"I'll come and talk to them."

"Will you? Will you really?" Her face lit up. She and the Colonel smiled warmly at one another and an idea came into Hansler's mind. But I'll sleep on it, he decided.

There was a heavy bump against the front door, as if some large body had struck it. The two men looked at Diana inquiringly.

"I don't know what that is," she said frowning. "I don't think it's the boggart—it's some animal that's been prowling around lately."

She took her shotgun from a corner, pulled up the window sash a couple of inches, thrust out the barrel, and fired. The sound of the explosion was deafening inside the cottage, and the room filled with blue smoke. "That usually scares it away," Diana said, leaning the gun back in its corner. "Would you like a little more coffee—or some bread and cheese?"

156

"No, we must really be getting along."

"I'd better come down the track with you," she said, reaching for the gun again.

"No, thank you, my dear, I've got my service revolver with me. You lock yourself up tight."

"Good night, then."

"Good night."

Paul thought he saw a large animal—perhaps a dog?—bounding along on the other side of the hedge as they walked down the track. But it did not come near them.

All was silent when they reached home, with not a light showing. They went straight to bed.

It was warmer next morning, with a mist drifting in off the sea—silvery, the sun behind it. Hansler, having slept on his idea and still finding it a good one, was determined to voice it at once.

"The solution to that girl's problem is simple," he said, meeting the Colonel before breakfast. "She's in love."

"In love, my dear chap?"

"You often get manifestations of that kind around un-married girls, but usually when they're younger. Of course it's falling in love that's brought it on in her case—that, and perhaps this peculiar atmosphere down here."

"But who's she fallen in love with?"

"You, of course, my dear man. So you'd better marry her —the sooner the better."

When Hansler said these words such a beaming, efful-gent glow of happiness lit up the Colonel's face that it was as if a switch had been pressed.

"In love with me? Marry her? I'll go up there after breakfast."

He sat down as if, for the moment, his legs would not

hold him, gazing at his boiled egg. Presently he wiped his eyes a little.

Hansler, looking up, became aware that Miss de Reszke had come in and was thoughtfully picking the dead flowers off a potted hyacinth on the windowsill.

"Have you fed the pigs yet?" she asked her brother lightly.

"Good lord, no—I forgot all about them." He jumped up and almost ran from the room. They heard him whistling, loud and sweet, in the scullery as he pulled on his boots.

"You must have an interesting practice, Mr. Hansler. I can see you're a very clever man," said Miss de Reszke, smiling, pouring coffee. A beam of sunshine, struggling through the mist, fell across the table, and she preened herself in it.

"No more interesting than your life, I imagine," Hansler said, smiling back at her, but he was aware of a little doubt beneath his gallantry.

There was a tremendous crash, as the Colonel flung the back door open again and came bursting in.

"What's the matter, my dear?" his sister asked. "You're quite white."

He made no reply, but went to the telephone and started dialing.

"Pig department? Give me the Inspector, please," he said. "That you, Curtis? Pevensey Jones here. God damn it, Curtis, twenty of my best sows have been killed—all had their throats torn out. That beast somehow made a hole in the breeze-block wall and got into the piggery. You'll have to come along and view the carcasses. Right? As soon as you can, yes."

There was a ping as he rang off, and he turned and looked at them. He was still quivering with rage.

"The—the *effrontery* of it!" he said.

## The Green Flash

"How sickening for you, my dear," his sister said sympathetically. "I always wondered if those breeze-block walls were really very strong."

The Colonel gulped down his coffee without replying. Then he said, "Betty, will you do something for me?"

"Of course, my dear."

"I promised Diana I'd go up to Treloe this morning and talk to the Committee for her. I shan't be able to go now—have to wait for Curtis. But you could go—you'd be just as good. It's quite simple—just tell them that I'm going to marry her and take over the farm—they've never taken any exception to my methods."

She showed no surprise, but inclined her head again, the half-smile curving up into her cheek.

"Mr. Hansler had better come too," she said.

"Yes, Paul, you go along too, my dear fellow. Tell her how sorry I am I couldn't come—she'll understand when she hears about the pigs. I'll be up this afternoon, say."

"We'll go around by way of Losthope," Miss de Reszke said, getting out the car after breakfast. "I want to match this green silk and get a new pair of gloves—these ones are quite worn through at the fingertips, see? with all the driving I do."

Somehow the errands in the shops of Losthope seemed to take much longer than Hansler had expected. Although Miss de Reszke appeared so decided she could not make up her mind about the exact shade of green; matching it entailed many trips with scraps of material to the light of the street, and back to the counter. Then, choosing the gloves was a difficult problem—should they be warm, fur-lined ones, which would last very well, or something thinner, suitable for coming summer? Hansler was fascinated by the sight of her hands, snugly encased in the fur gloves; he leaned on the counter beside her and stroked the fur delicately with his fingertip. She turned her head slowly and gave him a measuring, friendly look.

"Just fancy my brother getting married to Diana," she said. "Who will look after me? You must come and give me good advice from time to time, Mr. Hansler."

"There's nothing I'd like—" he began.

"And now if you'll excuse me, I must just go in here and do some trying-on of a more intimate kind, which I can't ask your advice on, just yet—" she said with a brilliantly confidential smile and gesture, as she vanished into a cubicle behind a green curtain, escorted by a saleswoman. Paul sat down patiently on a little thin-stalked chair to wait for her. The atmosphere of the shop was close, with its thick carpet, curtains, and ranks of garments everywhere on hangers; he wished she would hurry. She seemed to be taking a terribly long time.

At last she reappeared, exclaimed in contrition, and insisted on his having a drink to restore him.

"It won't take a moment, it's just here."

He followed her rapidly gliding figure into the hotel, where she engaged him in a long inquisition about his methods of work.

"My dear," she said, suddenly interrupting herself and glancing at her watch, "You *have* kept me talking. You must hurry, or we shall be too late for that poor girl."

He prepared himself for another of her lightning drives, but she said that the brake-blocks were giving trouble, and took the long climb up to the moor with greater care than she had hitherto displayed.

"Wait a moment!" Hansler exclaimed in excitement at a crossroads. "Wasn't that Diana on a motorbike?"

"Nonsense, my dear, what an imagination you have. She

has a motorbike, to be sure, but we know that she is at home see-ing the Committee, so it couldn't possibly have been she, could it?"

Hansler could not be certain, but he was anxious; that tense, despairing figure on the battered old machine hurtling off across the moor had been enough like Diana to trouble him, and he sat silent and frowning as they crept, in bottom gear, up the last steep length of track.

The house was empty. At first they thought the place was totally deserted; then, around at the back, they came on three little men in glasses, like owls, thoughtfully prodding at a piece of broken drainpipe that protruded from the ground.

"We've come to tell you that Colonel Pevensey Jones is taking over the farm from Miss Grieve," said Miss de Reszke, approaching them. They blinked at her.

"Can't do that, ma'am. Miss Grieve has already been dispossessed. In fact she's left. Of course the farm will be put up for auction, and the Colonel can bid for it then if he likes. Now if you'd come up here a couple of hours ago—"

"Oh dear," said Miss de Reszke. "How unfortunate. Can you tell me where Miss Grieve has gone?"

"Can't say, miss. The young lady was rather upset—offended, like. When we told her she'd been dispossessed and would have to quit at once she just ran and got out her motor-bike and went off on it. Of course by rights we should have stopped her, as the bike is included in the stock of the farm, which is all forfeit, as being part of a substandard enterprise. But you can't be too hard, and in any case we couldn't very well have stopped her."

"No indeed," said Miss de Reszke. "Well, this is all very sad. We had better go back and tell my brother. He'll be upset, I'm afraid."

# THE GREEN FLASH

Colonel Pevensey Jones was more than upset.

"Gone?" he said. "You mean you got there too late? Which way did she go?"

"I think she seemed to be going north," Hansler said miserably.

Without a word the Colonel went out to the scullery and began pulling on his boots.

"Where are you going?" his sister asked.

"Going to find her, of course. You can stay and look after the pigs for me till I get back, can't you, Hansler? There's a chap coming in to build a concrete wall this afternoon."

"How long do you suppose you'll be?"

"My dear chap, how can I possibly say? She's got a start on me, and can go much faster. But I'm going to find her."

He hurried off, and a moment later they heard the stuttering roar of the tractor starting, and saw him chug off up the road to the north.

"Oh well," said Miss de Reszke, "I'm glad you're here to keep me company."

She gave Paul an enigmatic look, and he smiled uneasily back. The house seemed unaccountably empty without the Colonel's trim, bouncing figure, and he was relieved to be able to spend the afternoon helping the bricklayer with the heavily reinforced wall at the back of the piggery.

By the time this was finished and the pigs were fed it was nearly sunset. Hansler strolled to the top of the garden, thinking with affection of his friend. Where was the Colonel now? Still chugging indomitably along some upland road? Or had he found Diana, was he perhaps with her on the summit of the moor, watching like Paul for the sun to go down?

Gradually the dark line of the sea inched across the

golden sphere until there was only a segment left—a line—a speck—

Hansler turned, stumbling, and ran back to the house.

"Miss de Reszke! Betty!" he shouted. "I saw it—the green flash! Oh, do you suppose he saw it too—"

He burst into her study and then stood perfectly still, frozen in the doorway.

From the middle of the room a large gray wolf looked back at him with pale and brilliant eyes.

## About the Book

Many of the stories in this collection were produced during a period that Joan Aiken worked for Argosy magazine. Her job limited long-term writing time, and since the magazine published exclusively short stories, she had a ready market for her work.

"Actually," Miss Aiken says, "I love short stories; my father Conrad Aiken has written such marvelous ones—his *Mr. Arcularis* and *Silent Snow, Secret Snow* are classics in the fantasy/horror genre—that I was bound to be influenced by them, and then, working on Argosy, I had unlimited opportunity to read all the cream of what was being published at that time, notably J. D. Salinger, Katherine Ann Porter, Elizabeth Bowen, Elizabeth Enright, Ray Bradbury, Hortense Calisher, Rhys Davies."

The fourteen tales in THE GREEN FLASH were chosen from among Miss Aiken's particular favorites. They cover a time span of almost twenty-five years. *The Dreamers* was the first, written in 1947 and published in the *New Statesman* in 1954. *Smell*, written in 1968, is the most recent.

77072-3